A Thousand Cherry Trees

A Novel By Shandy Lawson

Dauntless Books

A Thousand
Cherry Trees

Chapter 1

When I was in fourth grade I wrote a report on George Washington.

The story goes, when he was a boy young George was given a hatchet, which at the time was apparently the most amazing gift *ever,* and was also somehow an appropriate gift for a six-year-old. He went around the yard chopping at everything he saw, from weeds in the garden to fence posts. His parents thought it was adorable. But eventually he ran out of stuff to chop down, and that's when he spotted his father's favorite cherry tree.

The tree was strong and tall, not that cherry trees are all that huge to begin with, but to six-year-old George, it would have towered over him. He couldn't resist the challenge, and he went to work on it.

Later that day his father came home to see the tree lying dead in the yard. He was *beyond* pissed, and demanded to know who did such a terrible thing.

George, shaking with fear, came forward. "I cannot tell a lie, Pa," he said. "I cut down the cherry tree."

His father was so proud of his son for admitting the truth despite the fear of looming punishment that he completely let George off the hook. "Your honesty is worth more than a thousand cherry trees," he told George as he took him up in his arms, and everything was super and warm and lovely.

Such a sweet story.

Except the thing is it never happened. Sure, the Washington family may have had cherry trees on their property, and it's even possible that wee George was in possession of a hatchet–though giving a child a sharp little axe is crappy parenting, if you ask me. But this particular tale was probably lifted from a series of fictional stories from England that Washington's biographer had read in his youth.

Does it matter if the story isn't true? It's a good parable, regardless.

Maybe so many people have told and retold that story that by now it's *become* true. It happens. Like carpet odor didn't exist until they started selling carpet deodorizer. That's an actual fact. But now carpet odor obviously *does* exist, because you can buy stuff to get rid of it–and plenty of people do. Enough people believed the lie that it has become the truth.

Is truth just marketing then?

I only bring this up because you might hear some conflicting stories about what really went on in Burnham in the summer of 1989, and it's important that you keep in mind the way the truth can be *pliable*.

Madison, James
Mejias/San Diego County/CA
6/27/89 12:35 hrs

    Det. K. Ferrara
    Det. M. Perez

KF: This interview of James Madison is being recorded for the purpose of the investigation into the... into the Burnham matter. We're in the East Interview Room at the State Police headquarters building in the city of Mejias, California. I'm Detective Keith Ferrara, also present here is Detective Miguel Perez, and also we have James's father, David Madison in the room with us as well. The date is the 27th of June, 1989. The time is 12:35 PM.

    [Inaudible]

    KF: First things first. We'll get to that, Mike.

    MP: Okay.

    KF: Could you please state your name and your date of birth.

    JM: My name is James Lewis Madison, and my birthday is May 12, 1973.

    KF: So you're... sixteen years old.

    JM: Yes.

    KF: And your address?

    JM: 812 Crowder Street, apartment D, Boston, Massachusetts.

KF: Okay, thank you James. This interview is being tape recorded so that in the event that this matter ends up in a courtroom, this tape can be used in evidence, should it come to that. Do you understand what I'm telling you?

JM: Uh-huh.

KF: That was a yes?

JM: Yes. I understand.

KF: Okay, good. Good then. Are you comfortable James, do you need to use the restroom or anything before we get started?

JM: No, I'm good.

KF: Great, okay. How's... I see you're pretty bandaged up there, how's your arm?

JM: It's fine.

KF: For the record, you were hospitalized for that, and you were just discharged this morning, um, hospitalized immediately following all that business out by Route 48, is that correct?

JM: That's correct.

KF: Just the one night in the hospital.

JM: Right.

KF: Well, um, thank you for coming right out to see us so soon after your discharge. It was certainly a traumatic couple of days for you I'm sure.

JM: It was.

KF: Well, hopefully we can begin to put all of that behind us, and the first step is this interview right here. Now, James, are you currently on any medications, like pain medications, that might impair your ability to be accurate in your telling of the events that transpired over the last—

JM: Yeah, I'm fine. No pain medication, just the Amoxicillin.

KF: And that's an antibiotic, for the wound.

JM: Right.

KF: Okay, great. Now... can you start at the beginning? I guess I mean around the time you first came to town.

JM: When I met Sunny.

KF: Okay, why don't you tell us about Sunny.

Chapter 2

I watched her glide past the end of each aisle in the tiny general store, disappearing for a moment only to reappear as she moved past the next aisle over. The soles of her shoes whispered over the ancient linoleum floor as she passed rows of canned soup, motor oil and magazines. I mirrored her casual pace as I walked through the front of the store and she walked through the back, and she stopped when she came to the aisle where they sold the hunting and fishing stuff.

She was tall, a good two or three inches taller than me, with dark hair and freckles. Bright green eyes. Her fingers played over a little plastic box of polished steel balls, ammo for a slingshot. I remembered they used to sell them here, the modern steel slingshots with the wrist support and everything–some of the old-timers actually hunted with them. She pulled the box from the shelf and slid it neatly into her front pocket.

She looked up and caught me watching her, and for a second I panicked: I've never been a witness to a crime before. But as our eyes met, her face expressionless, almost *cold*–she winked.

The endless plane of the California desert swallowed me up the moment I stepped through the door as I followed her outside and into the blazing heat of the gravel parking lot, though she hadn't really invited me to do so. The wink maybe, there was something about it that made me want to go after her, but I couldn't say why. Just drawn to her, I guess.

She sat on one of the picnic tables next to the front door, sat up on top of it with her sneakers on the bench part, and leaned forward, elbows on her knees. She squinted into the sun and tilted her head to one side as I approached, sizing me up. "You like, store security or something? Loss Prevention?" she asked.

I wasn't sure what to say. I looked back at the entry to the general store, the little place no bigger inside than a tennis court, with its one owner and three employees. Surely she was kidding; a place that small would never have a loss prev—

"Or is it bigger than that? Is this a *sting?* Are you state police?" She paused and shook her head. "No... no, you don't have a mustache. Must be federal then. Some kind of *narc.*" She slid off the picnic table and stood so our noses were inches apart. "So what would Uncle Sam want with me, then? Is this about...wait. Is this about those murders up in Palm Springs?"

She took a step back, her eyes filling with fear, her body tense as though ready to run. But just as suddenly, her gaze narrowed until it was fixed firmly on my own, our eyes locked together and I couldn't look away. "*I'll kill you if you try to take turn me in,*" she whispered.

I swallowed loudly, my throat dry and my palms wet. She doubled over in laughter, collapsing onto the bench, nearly in tears. "Oh my God...I was kidding, you tool. Jesus, you should see your face..."

I took a seat next to her, drying my hands on my jeans. "You scared the hell out of me."

"Yeah, no shit. You're pale and everything." Another round of laughter from the girl with the green eyes and pocketful of stolen ammo. She wiped a tear from one eye with the back of her hand. "It's good to see a new face around here. I'm Sunny."

I looked out into the desert, the low afternoon sun casting the hills, everything, in gold. My heartbeat eventually returned to a reasonable pace and I offered a smile. "James," I said.

"Hello, Mr. James."

I glanced at the rectangular outline of the plastic box in her front pocket. "So what's with the ammo?"

She cocked her head and knitted her brow as though I'd asked the stupidest question she'd ever heard. "It's to go with the slingshot I stole this morning. *Duh.*"

* * *

I followed her across the parking lot to the main road—or I should say the *only* road—the only one important enough to have a name, anyway: *Route 48*. My dad's house was about a mile north, to our right, as were most homes in Burnham. I expected her to go that way too, but instead she walked across the street towards a rough road cut into the desert, a trail perpendicular to Route 48 that only led to one place and no further.

"You live in the Dropouts?" I asked her.

She nodded, smirking. "Is that a problem?"

"No, I just—no, that's cool. My dad lives up that way." I gestured to the right, where the main road curled against a jagged rise of rocky outcroppings with a few mailbox posts dotting the way. Three or four stucco homes with terra cotta roofs were visible before the street disappeared behind a steep hill of rock and dry brush.

"Hang out tomorrow?" Sunny asked.

I answered, "Sure," but she may not have heard me as she walked into the sun, kicking up a trail of dust, down the road to the little makeshift town in the valley about a mile away.

Chapter 3

Walking along the main road back to Dad's house, it occurred to me how little Burnham has changed since I'd been here last. Three years is a long time, and while I've changed a lot, this town is *exactly* the same.

Almost.

The sand still crept into the road at the bottom of the hill that led up to most of the houses here, and skinny Mr. Croxley–who volunteered for the job–still swept the sand back where it belonged in the morning with his red-handled push broom. All the houses I'd seen were the same color they'd been since my earliest memories, and even the few cars that passed by were familiar.

The *air* was the same. Dry. Hot.

Burnham had long ago found its balance, its perfect state, and there was no reason to change. Nobody ever left here, nobody ever arrived here. Except for Sunny.

Besides her, everything was the same, which meant everything was *boring*.

Most of the year I lived in Boston with my mom where we had tall buildings, good restaurants, things to *do*. The town of Burnham, California has never had any of those things.

Let me take that back: I'm not sure if it

qualified as a *restaurant*, but there was a pretty awesome Mexican breakfast and lunch spot in Burnham. *La Cocina.* Half the place was a market, sort of a convenience store (but even smaller than the general store closer to Dad's house), and the other half was a long counter with those stools that spun and a menu board I couldn't read because none of it was in English. But that was the only food for twenty miles, until you got to Mejias, which was another small town, but in Mejias they had a motel, a State Police barracks and a twenty-four hour medical emergency clinic—so compared to Burnham it might as well have been all five boroughs of New York City.

If you want to find Burnham on a map, first find San Diego, then look north-northeast for a big empty spot about halfway between San Diego and Palm Springs. That's where Burnham lies, but you won't actually see it on the map because towns with only a hundred and forty people living in them aren't generally map-worthy. You might find the main road, but even *that* doesn't appear on half the maps I've seen.

The town of Burnham isn't on the way to *anywhere*. Nobody ever had a reason to pass through. There's one main drag, Route 48, which runs through town, with seven or eight dead-end cross-streets on which most of the residents live. It's not a straight road, it curves around rock formations nobody felt like blasting flat, and rises and dips as it gains elevation on its way north toward Palm Springs.

It used to be, well—not quite a city, but it used to be bigger. There was a silver boom there in the 1860's, and it made a few people rich. Just a few got lucky in the mining game, but with sudden riches come a whole bunch of other people who will try to cash in too. Half the people who arrived came to look for silver in the ground, and the other half went into business to fill the need for saloons, tailors, lawyers, laborers. The mine stopped producing after fifteen years or so, and most of those newcomers left for other towns that still had silver in them. Or better yet, gold.

The original mine is still open, though only as a tourist attraction (there's even a gift shop, open Monday mornings from nine to eleven—or by appointment) but I can't imagine more than a handful of people actually going out there just to see an empty old mineshaft. I'm a history freak, and even *I* got bored there.

Now, a hundred and forty people live in the sixty-two homes, miles and miles from anywhere else in the southern Californian desert. And that's sixty-two homes if you don't count the Dropouts.

Which no one ever did.

Sixty-two homes with the same flowers planted in the same place next to the same car in the same driveway, year after year. Nothing changed, never ever.

Until Sunny arrived.

* * *

In the spring of 1971 a woman named Gwen, along with her husband Raymond, arrived in Burnham in a brown Plymouth station wagon. They'd come all the way from their home in Wilmington, Delaware, driving for three days straight.

Wilmington had not been kind to either of them, both having lost their jobs only a week apart, and they'd already been two months behind on the rent as it was. The winter had been a long one, and to save money they'd kept the heat turned down all night and turned it off altogether during the day. Once, Raymond came home from work to find the toilet had iced over. Or so the story goes.

Admitting defeat, they'd packed most of their clothes, whatever food remained in the cupboards, and a stack of books, piling it all in their car and simply drove away, giving their drafty old apartment the finger as they pulled away from the curb.

Four days later they'd gone as far as they could go. Upon reaching Burnham (they'd wandered away from the highway long ago—their ultimate destination is said to have been some beach in Baja) the car ran out of gas, but not before the fan belt broke, the muffler fell off, and a slow leak in one of the tires made speeds over forty nearly impossible. When the engine sputtered for the very last time, Gwen pointed the station wagon off the road and down a hill, coasting as far as they could. When they finally eased to a stop, they'd rolled a full mile off Route 48.

Raymond and Gwen stepped out of the car, stretched like cats just waking from a nap, and began to unpack. They had just become the founders and first residents of the Dropouts.

Their home became that blue Plymouth station wagon. It was where they spent the day keeping out of the sun and where they slept during the night. Their few belongings were stashed under the car or piled on the dashboard to keep the sun from coming through the windshield. They'd arrived with a little over forty dollars between them, and Neil gave them a discount at the general store on nonperishable items like pasta and canned soup. He let them fill their water jugs from the spigot around back.

When it was clear that Raymond and Gwen meant to stay, a few of Burnham's residents stopped by with supplies. A lot of it was stuff that would normally have ended up in the trash, but Raymond and Gwen found the old tarps, buckets, ropes and tent stakes quite useful. The Burnham folks were friendly.

Not everyone in town was so kind however, and the story goes that "the Dropouts" was not the name given to the community that rose from the desert out there by that old blue Plymouth, but instead was used by some when referring to Raymond and Gwen themselves, to how they'd simply thrown in the towel and abandoned modern life altogether.

Enough people had pointed westward towards the couple living in their car while saying *the dropouts* that that whole part of the desert took on the name.

Word of a stubborn pair of easterners who rejected the obligations and limitations of modern society reached nearby towns and further cities and soon a few more people moved into tents or campers next to Raymond and Gwen. As the tiny community grew, it became less a place to *escape* the pressures of the modern age and more a place to embrace freedom. A resident of the Dropouts didn't have to worry about paying rent, getting to work on time, or paying taxes. They didn't even have to wear clothes if they didn't want to, and more than a few didn't want to.

Raymond died suddenly in 1979 after living in the Dropouts for eight years. He was working to install a new well pump (they hadn't drank from the spigot at the general store since '75 and they were damned proud of it) and collapsed right there on top of his toolbox. It was a stroke, a former surgeon and provisional Dropouts doctor had said. There was nothing to be done for him—he was unconscious and Gwen sensed his spirit had left his body a while ago. So he lay in the Plymouth, his home, her home, and he passed away twenty-four hours later.

At the time, there were thirty-one permanent residents in the Dropouts, and as they buried him out past the northern boundary of the camp, everyone held smoking branches from low-growing desert scrub instead of candles and told stories about times when Raymond had made them laugh.

Gwen had always been a natural leader, the unofficial elder of the community, and after the death of Raymond, the nickname Mother Gwen grew and stuck. Nobody had ever bothered to make any rules there (nor would anyone have bothered to follow them), and there was no system of law or even an accepted code of ethics—but if anyone was looked to as a guiding hand in morality and how to *live proper*, it was Mother Gwen.

Chapter 4

Even if it was ninety degrees during the day, nights could still get chilly out in the desert, so dad made a lot of stuff like beef stew, shepherd's pie, you know—cold-weather food. It didn't really get *that* cold, but one of the things Dad missed about living in New England with mom and me was the food. The heavy, one-pot winter meals. Tonight we were having my favorite—mac and cheese—to celebrate my first night back in Burnham.

"Ready for another summer in paradise?" Dad pulled our dinner out of the oven and shut the door with his foot.

I nodded. While most kids I knew spent the week with one parent and the weekend with the other, my dad had to live three thousand miles away. So I got my whole year's worth of dad-time in one shot, for three months each summer. He worked from home writing freelance pieces for financial magazines, so he was always around, which was kind of cool. Handy if I needed a lift somewhere.

"Mrs. McCarthy's cat still comes to the back door sometimes," he said. "Still looking for dinner scraps."

Every night I used to put leftovers from dinner in a little bowl on the back porch for the neighbor's cat, a thin little calico named Belle. She'd purr and take a timeout from eating only long enough to glance up at me with what I interpreted as gratitude, maybe even affection. I grew pretty attached to that cat over the years.

He dropped a half-pound of the stuff on my plate, and we sat facing each other at the tiny dinner table in one end of the kitchen. "Seen Dayle yet?" Dad asked me.

I shook my head. "Went by the store this afternoon but she wasn't working. Probably see her tomorrow."

"Well, you've only been in town for half a day. She'll be happy to see you. It's been, what—three years?"

Yup, the last time I'd seen Dayle we were thirteen. I used to come out here and spend every summer with my dad, and most of that time was spent with Dayle. For such a boring little town, we always found plenty of trouble to get into together.

But a few summers ago Mom and Dad started fighting again, even though they hadn't even seen each other since I was little. Probably they fought over money—I couldn't imagine what else they'd have to fight about. I'd had to stay in Boston with Mom for the last three summers while they worked it out, so I hadn't seen dad in forever.

"She still send you those letters?" Dad asked behind a forkful of macaroni. He always thought it was so cute, Dayle and I swapping letters throughout the year while I was back home.

"Nah," I mumbled. "Not since a couple summers ago."

We ate in silence except for the occasional *clink* of forks against ceramic, the *thunk* of glasses hitting the table. It was weird, all this quiet. Back home, Mom always had the TV on when we ate dinner. Sometimes we'd talk, but it was nice knowing we didn't *have* to. We could always just stare at the TV instead.

Dad cleared his throat like he was going to say something, then didn't.

Clink, thunk.

"Hey, remember we used to have our Daily Fact?" Dad was talking about our old dinnertime ritual. Each night while we ate dinner, I'd provide a fact from whatever era of history I was into at the time. Sometimes we'd get talking about it until nine or ten o'clock.

I thought for a moment. "The ancient Romans used human urine as mouthwash," I offered.

"You're kidding."

"Nope."

"That's absolutely disgusting," Dad said. He tried not to laugh but it still slipped out a little.

"It's all I had on short notice," I said.

"Maybe tomorrow night we go with something a little less...biological."

I thought that was probably a good idea.

"Met a girl who lives in the Dropouts today," I said.

"Oh?" Dad had the typical opinion of those living in the Dropouts: they were probably decent people, hippies to be sure, but harmless enough as long as they kept to themselves. They didn't venture into town much, except to shop at the general store or sell stuff they made or grew at the farmers market on Sundays.

"Her name's Sunny," I said.

"She gonna be your Dayle this year?"

I laughed. "Doubt it. She's...weird. I don't know."

"Your age?"

"I think so. Maybe a year older. Seventeen, probably."

"You should take her out past the valley and show her the Buick, if she hasn't found it on her own yet."

"I doubt she'd be blown away by an abandoned car stuck in the sand, Dad."

Dad chuckled. "You never know what will impress a girl, James. I'm halfway through my forties and I'll be damned if I've got it figured out."

Impressing women was a skill I ranked up there with juggling chainsaws and performing heart transplants. It'd be an awesome tool to have, but I wasn't going to hold my breath waiting for it to appear on my workbench.

Dad pointed his fork at me with a crooked

grin. "Well, don't you two get into any trouble, now."

* * *

After dinner I went down the hall to my room and unpacked the two suitcases I'd brought with me. Each bag was stuffed with an equal mix of clothes and books; layers were important, since the days can be insanely hot but the nights can be chilly, and without the distractions of the city to keep me busy, I figured I'd be doing a *lot* of reading over the next few months.

The books were there to supplement the ones I already had in my bedroom. Dad hadn't touched my room since I was last here, and the books he'd given me for my birthdays and Christmases (we celebrated Christmas in July, since we never saw each other in December) still lined the bookshelf that reached almost to the ceiling.

Dad used to give me toys as gifts: radio controlled trucks, video games, stuff he saw other kids my age spending their time with. But books were all I ever asked for, so eventually that was all he ever gave me.

I didn't want just any kind of book though—there was no fiction on my shelf. My thing was history. Specifically I was into American history, and to be *really* specific I liked to read about the Revolution and the founding fathers. Maybe a little civil war now and then.

But any kind of history would do, I wasn't picky. On the plane in from Boston the night before I'd read a great little paperback about the French Revolution, which I'd started to get into—that period is loaded with great characters, but more importantly, lots of irony. Any good history book is packed with irony and bad decisions. Did you know the guy who invented the guillotine was executed with one?

History is loaded with people who suffered ironic deaths like that. Fred Duesenberg, of Duesenberg automobiles, was killed while driving a Duesenberg automobile. Horace Hunley, inventor of the first combat submarine, died in his invention when it failed to resurface and he and his crew drowned. And you can probably guess what happened to the chief architect of the RMS Titanic.

It happens all the time: people are done in by the things they create. And lying in bed that night, I wondered what I was going to create and if it would come after me. I figured I was pretty safe, being a student of history—it's not like I was trying to invent some new fire-retardant suit that I could end up burning to death in or anything. At best, maybe I'd write a book or two, and probably teach for a while.

If I taught, I'd have to keep a wary eye on my students.

I rolled over, trying to think about

something a little less grim.

Like girls.

I'd really been looking forward to seeing Dayle this summer, but the unexpected appearance of this new girl, Sunny, might make things interesting.

Chapter 5

When we were eleven years old, Dayle and I got caught in a dust storm. I'd always heard about them, mostly from stories the old folks told around the general store, tales of brown clouds, sometimes black ones, and they moved across the desert like a massive wall stretching thousands of feet up into the sky. But I'd never seen anything like that myself.

I'd seen *pictures* of course, grainy old photos in my books back home. For a while I was into that little slice of American history between World War I and World War II, where so much happened that often gets overlooked. Like the Dustbowl, when farmers overplanted and cleared away all the grass, and that combined with a drought to turn part of the Midwest into a giant sandbox. The wind swept all that dry soil up and carried it along, turning the sky black and building up static electricity that charged wire fences and electrocuted wandering rabbits. Whole farms were swallowed up by the sand and dust, and people died from breathing it all in.

I'd built a diorama for a school project once, about the Great Depression and the Dustbowl. My diorama had a tiny little farmhouse half-buried in dirt, just the tops of fence posts poking out of the soil because the rest had been consumed by a duster.

I even made a little cow skeleton out of white electrical wire and laid it on its side in the yard to show how the livestock were often wiped out from swallowing all that dirt in the air. Most of the other kids did their projects about Native Americans, because it was easy to make a teepee out of construction paper.

The day had started just like any other, sunny and bright. Hot. We spent most of the day in Dayle's pool, only getting out long enough to devour a couple of peanut butter and jelly sandwiches and a handful of chips. *No food in the pool,* her dad always said, otherwise we probably wouldn't have gotten out, ever.

By three o'clock that afternoon we were exhausted, our fingers and toes wrinkly and our bodies drained of every last bit of energy. Seven straight hours of pool play can take a lot out of you.

We decided to head over to my house, to hang out on the couch and be lazy. Dad had bought me an Atari for our Christmas in July, which I wasn't really into, but Dayle flipped out over it so it was usually a pretty good way to pass an afternoon.

The only game I was good at was *Yars Revenge*. And sometimes I was okay at *Combat*, that slow one with the tanks.

We were halfway between her house and mine, walking along the side of Route 48, when the sky turned brown. The wind kicked up suddenly, and it got dark, like the time of night when Dad usually called me inside. Not like actual *nighttime,* but almost. It was a weird kind of dark, because the sun was still up there, diffused by this giant black cloud approaching Burnham. The light that managed to filter through seemed to come from all around us, casting no shadows.

At first the dust in the air was just an irritation. I rubbed my eyes with one knuckle and Dayle did too, and a minute or two later we each coughed a couple of times. But before I could suggest we pull our shirts up and try to breathe through them like a mask, the cloud was on us.

The static in the air made the hair on my arms and neck stand up, and through the roar of the wind I heard Dayle cry out. I kept my eyes almost closed, just the narrowest of slits to see through, and grabbed her hand so we wouldn't get separated.

The sand coated our eyes, and all the tears in the world wouldn't flush any of it out. If anything, our tears made it worse, it gave the dust something to stick to. We just squeezed our eyes shut, our tee-shirts over our mouths, the flying sand stinging every exposed inch of us.

I felt pavement under my sneakers, and with my hand in Dayle's, I shuffled until I found the edge of the road. I got us as far from the blacktop as I could so we wouldn't get run over if anyone tried to drive on through the storm, and I crouched next to her against a Joshua tree. I pulled my shirt off and wrapped it around Dayle's head, covering her face. My exposed back and ribs burned with every gust of wind.

With both arms around her, I felt her sobbing and gasping for breath. I'd never realized how tiny she was before, but right then it felt like I could have scooped her up like a bundle of laundry. I buried my face in her hair—it didn't do much to filter out the sand but it was better than nothing. Mostly, I held my breath when I could.

The storm had started quickly, but it seemed to take forever to wind down. The wind died little by little, much of the dust still suspended in the air even after the winds had passed on far to the southeast. I kept my arm around Dayle and we walked to the general store so we could both flush out our eyes with water. Tears cut clean trails down our cheeks.

After we'd washed our eyes and mouths out (the feeling of all that grit between my teeth will stay with me forever) Shelby gave us a couple of sodas for free.

She'd watched us come in, my shirt still looped around Dayle's neck, my arm over her shoulder, and said to Dayle, "You have a special friend there, looking out for you like that. Be a cold day in hell before my husband gave me his shirt in a dust storm."

Dayle looked at me and smiled. "I guess James is okay, once you get over the smell."

I pretended to punch her arm, and she pretended to punch my ribs, which actually hurt for real from the sandblasting my skin had taken. She gasped, said she was sorry, and let her head fall sideways on my shoulder. "You're right, though," she said to Shelby. "I should probably keep him."

"Well if you don't, I might just snatch him up," Shel said with a wink.

* * *

Sunny was waiting for me when I got to the General Store, sitting on the same picnic table as the day before. "You're late," she said.

"You never told me what time to meet you."

"That's no excuse."

I couldn't help smiling as I passed by her. "Give me a sec, I gotta get something inside." I jogged up the wide front steps and opened the door, the bell that hung overhead tinkling as I came in.

I went to the counter and saw Shelby there, greeting me with a feigned heart attack, clutching her chest in shock.

"You're all grown *up*." She said it as though she were trying to convince me. "*Look* at you."

"Hey Shel." Shelby's worked in the general store ever since I could remember. She was around Dad's age and always felt like an aunt to me—she'd keep an eye on me and make sure I stayed out of trouble, but then slip me a pack of firecrackers when Dad wasn't looking. She was cool.

"You're looking for Dayle," she said.

I nodded. "She working today? I came by yesterday, but—"

Shelby jerked a thumb over her shoulder. "Out back on her break. I bet she'll be excited to see you."

I passed potato chips, cat food and motor oil on my way to the back door, and fumbled nervously with the doorknob, trying to figure out what to say when I made my surprise appearance. I decided to see where Dayle's reaction took me and go from there. Don't want to *over*-plan an entrance or it'll come off rehearsed.

I pushed the door open, my shoulders back, standing up straight, my best casual smile at the ready. I was met with a tiny dark closet with a grimy toilet centered in it.

"That's the shitter, hon," Shelby called from behind the counter. "Back door is to your left."

So it was. I closed the bathroom door and took three steps to the left and opened the correct one, my shoulders back, standing up straight, my best casual smile at the ready.

The sun wilted my smile immediately as I squinted from the sudden brightness. Dayle sat on the edge of what passed for the store's loading dock, an elevated wooden walkway the delivery trucks backed up to. A boy sat next to her, her hand in his, and they swung their feet back and forth over the edge. He wore a baseball hat that shaded his face from the sun.

I hopped down the steps, kicking up beige clouds of dust, immediately regretting going that way instead of taking the walkway over to her—as I now found myself eye-level with her knees, having to crane my neck upwards, squinting, to see her face.

Not how I'd imagined it going.

"Hey, Dayle," I said, probably too quietly.

"Oh—Jamie. Hey." She smiled at me, sort of. Not really. More of a fake smile, a polite and patient one. Instinctively I started to correct her, to say no one called me Jamie anymore, it was James now, but I faltered a few words in and let it go.

She was positioned perfectly so the sun was just behind her head, so if I wanted to see her face I had to shield my eyes with one hand and sort of move my head around in different directions until I got the sun behind her so I wouldn't be blinded. Even then, I could only look for the briefest moment before my eyes burned and I had to look down again.

A few moments of silence passed while I stared at her knees, then up at her face for just a second before looking away as though something on the horizon was *fascinating*. "You cut your hair," I said. It was short now, really short, like a boy's cut. It used to be light blonde and reached almost to her waist, now it was darker and cut almost like mine.

I bobbed my head around like a chicken,

trying to stay in the shadow of Dayle's head.

"Cut it like a year and a half ago," she said. I sensed disinterest.

I nodded like I'd known that but had forgotten, that I'd somehow gotten the news three thousand miles away that Dayle had cut her hair. Like I was really on top of things.

Not that I was dying to meet the kid she held hands with, but as I pretended to look for something in my pocket I sort of hoped she'd make the introduction just so there would be some words spoken to break the awkwardness. No such luck.

Finally I offered a weak wave. "I've got some stuff to do at Dad's, so I gotta take off..."

"'Kay," Dayle said. "My break's almost over anyway, so, you know."

Another weak wave. "Sure," I said. Big fake smile. "Maybe I'll see you around, or—"

"Sure, maybe," Dayle said. The guy next to her still hadn't said a word, and I felt like they both studied me as I walked away, up the steps and back into the store.

Chapter 6

"You're not really *smoking* if you don't *inhale* it," Sunny said. "If you don't inhale it, you're just being some poser wasting my cigarette."

We sat in the dappled shade of a Joshua tree away from the road, hidden from sight by a rise in the desert that paralleled route 48. She balanced the lighter crosswise on her index finger as she watched me, the sun making the bright blue plastic look electric.

I held the cigarette gingerly between two fingers, trying desperately, and unsuccessfully, to make it look natural. I drew in a cautious lungful of smoke and coughed immediately, managing to hand it off to her as I doubled over, hacking away.

"Maybe I need a different brand," I mumbled between coughing fits.

"Man, you suck at this," Sunny said. I nodded in agreement, suddenly queasy. "So what did you need at the store?" she asked.

I held back the urge to vomit, the taste of the cigarette inescapable, and spit into the dust. "A soda," I said.

Sunny gave me a quick look up and down, clearly noting I held no soda. "So how'd that work out?"

"Not very well."

"I've known you for a grand total of fifteen minutes, and so far you suck at smoking cigarettes and buying pop. Is there *anything* you're good at, or should we just sit quietly so you don't hurt yourself?"

I waved her off. "I'll be fine in a few." As I said this, I gagged.

"So what's your story?" she asked. "You're new here but you kinda know your way around."

"My dad lives here in Burnham. I used to spend every summer with him, but I haven't been out here in a few years. It hasn't changed much though. What about you? I don't remember ever seeing you around here before."

Sunny shrugged. "Been here since last June, so about a year. It's the typical story: my mom burned up in a fire that my dad set, and now I live by myself in an off-the-grid hippie commune in the California desert."

"Yeah, that old cliché," I said. "If I had a nickel for every time I heard that one, I'd have like... *one nickel.*"

"Actually," she said, "You wouldn't believe some of the weird shit that drove people to live out there." She nodded westward, toward the Dropouts. "Mostly people dodging child support or whatever, but there's no shortage of weird cases. I miss big soft beds and long hot showers and everything, but all in all it's pretty nice. It's...simple."

"So—" I wasn't sure if I should ask, but I was too curious. "Your *dad* killed your *mom?* As in murder?"

Sunny shrugged. "Well, maybe not exactly like that, it was technically manslaughter, I think. It was an accident, but still his fault. He drinks a lot, and he passed out one night in the living room downstairs with a cigarette in one hand and a pint of vodka in the other. *Whoosh*." She mimed flames rocketing into the sky.

"Jeez."

"Yeah. I was just coming home from a party when I saw the house on fire from up the street. Dad was in the front yard, trashed, just watching the place burn. Mom never even made it out of bed, they told me." She took a drag off her cigarette. "Died from the smoke."

I winced. "Sorry."

She shrugged again. "Shit happens. There wasn't a trial or anything, and the fire chief said it was an accident, so I guess it was an accident." She looked off toward the little valley, where the cluster of tents, teepees and broken-down RV's were arranged in an unlikely grid. "I took off with some clothes and cash, wandered a few days and ended up here. Dad said he wouldn't come looking for me if I promised I'd come back before school started in the fall. He was just afraid I'd run away for good, so he would've agreed to pretty much anything."

"You really going back in the fall?"

"Nah."

"And where's home, anyway?"

"San Diego. Well, La Mesa, but you know.

It's kind of all San Diego out there."

I didn't know, but I nodded like did.

Sunny offered me the last drag off her cigarette, which I declined as coolly as I could, before grinding it beneath her sneaker in the sand. She gazed far off, past the Dropouts, past whatever lay beyond, and put a friendly arm around my shoulder. "I think we're gonna have a good time, you know. This'll be an awesome summer. The summer of Sunny and James."

I couldn't help smiling, but as I did my thoughts flashed to the loading dock behind the store, to Dayle's total indifference at my triumphant return to Burnham. To her complete failure to notice how grown-up I'd become—I mean, even Shelby had seen how I looked different, better.

I'd been doing pushups and everything, back home in our apartment in Boston, every night. All for nothing.

I wondered if Sunny thought I looked like I'd been doing pushups every night in my apartment in Boston. Maybe if she'd seen me three years ago, when I was a lot smaller, for comparison's sake. Maybe she'd be impressed.

It would've been nice to impress *one* of them.

Chapter 7

The next morning, Dad called to me from his little office at the end of the hall, past my bedroom. "Breakfast is in the freezer," he said. "There's OJ in the fridge, too."

I opened the freezer to find five or six pounds of ground beef, a plastic bin of ice cubes that smelled like onions, and a box of frozen waffles. The cold air flowed down the front of the refrigerator door and over my bare feet. I let the door swing shut.

"I'll grab something later," I answered.

"Okey dokey."

"Hey," he called out. "You smelled like an ashtray when you came in yesterday. You're not smoking, are you?"

"No," I said. "It's Sunny."

"I don't have to worry about you, do I?"

"Trust me Dad, smoking's not my thing." My stomach did a flip just thinking about it. "You don't have to worry about me."

"You sure?"

It occurred to me that Dad never *had* worried about me. Even when Dayle and I would go out and wander around the desert, where there are snakes and who knows what else, along with the ever-present potential to wander too far and get lost

—he never worried.

Or, he never *told* me he worried, anyway.

Odd that he seemed to have decided to start now, when I was pretty much grown up.

"I'm sure," I answered.

As I left the house I heard dad typing away on his computer, working on a column for whatever financial paper or magazine he was freelancing for this month.

* * *

"Come on, don't be a wuss," Sunny said. "You wanna walk all the way there like a loser or ride in style like a *man?*"

I stared at the pickup, a big Ford from the '70's, with its chunky tires and fiberglass cap over the bed. "I don't know. I mean it's kind of a nice day for a walk," I replied.

She rolled her eyes. The truck idled in the last parking space next to the Dumpster in front of the general store, its owner inside, stocking up on whatever.

"This guy's going right back to the Dropouts," she said. "He lives like a hundred feet from my tent and never goes anywhere but back and forth from his RV to the store. I've done this at least twenty times since I've been here."

I knew the truck. I didn't know the owner's name, but I recognized the old Ford as belonging to a guy from the Dropouts, and Sunny was right—since I was a kid I'd never seen it anywhere but in the store parking lot or on the road down into the valley.

"I *know* you don't want to walk."

"It's only a mile," I said. "The walk down there's easy. Wouldn't take us more than twenty minutes." I didn't feel good about hiding in the back of a stranger's truck just to get a free lift a mile down the road. "Why don't we just *ask* the guy if we can ride in the back—"

"What's the fun in that? *Come on,*" she said. "You want to show me this stupid Toyota thing or what?"

"It's a Buick."

"A what?"

"It's a Buick, not a Toyota."

Sunny rolled her eyes. "Whatever. If you want to show me the Buick, then get your ass in the back of that truck."

I hesitated.

"Jesus *Christ.* It's ninety degrees and I'm not walking if I don't have to. The guy's been in the store for five minutes already, probably won't be in there much longer." Her gaze bore a hole in my brain as she twisted the lever on the truck's cap and swung the rear window up, then stepped up onto the bumper and lifted one leg inside, and then the other. From the relative darkness inside the truck she sighed loudly and said, "I'll show you a boob."

"Only one?" I asked, climbing in.

"I need to save the other for the return trip. You'll have to get home *somehow*."

* * *

It was a *great* boob.

* * *

After the truck pulled up in front of the owner's RV, we waited a couple of minutes in silence before slipping out onto the packed trail that ran the length of the Dropouts. They called it Main Street, the residents here, the dirt road that led arrow-straight from the east end of the dropouts to the west. And like Main Street in any other town, most of the village's bigger homes lined it while the smaller ones were nestled on the side streets running perpendicular to it. We passed RV's with tires that had gone flat years ago and large canvas multi-room tents anchored to the ground with heavy iron stakes. Clotheslines arced from the corner of one tent to the next. "Where's your tent?" I asked her.

Sunny waved vaguely over her shoulder. "Back that way," she said. "Where's this car?"

I pointed generally west. Somewhere nearby, somebody cooked chicken over a charcoal grill. The smoke drifted past us on the breeze, along with a few brief curses as the same somebody burned himself.

We walked out to the Buick, a car buried almost up to the tops of its tires in the desert about a half-mile west of the Dropouts. The Buick had been left there at least twenty years ago, probably longer—even the local old-timers couldn't pin a year on when it had first appeared there. It was a '58 Special, painted sort of an olive green, and it blended pretty well with the colors of the desert. Though it sat only a hundred yards or so off the side of the road it was easily overlooked, partly obscured by a knotty Joshua tree.

The Buick cast unnatural shadows on the desert floor, straight lines and smooth arcs from the quarter-panels and roof, the only evidence of human influence for as far as the eye could see, when looking from the west. The sand curled around it in frozen waves, rising slowly to meet the sheet metal of its fenders and bumpers only to drop away suddenly before making contact.

"Okay, I guess this is pretty cool," Sunny said. "I wonder how it got buried like that."

"Dad says somebody just abandoned it here in the sixties and the desert sort of grew around it. It was here even before the Dropouts were. But wait —it gets cooler." I took a few steps back and picked up a baseball-sized rock. "Back up a bit."

Sunny stood next to me and watched as I tossed the stone in a high arc, her gaze following it through the air as it landed with a loud *thunk* on the Buick's hood. Instantly the sound of rattles erupted from inside the car as a puff of dust rose where the rock had struck the paint, and Sunny's eyes lit up like she had flashlights behind them.

"Whoa," she said, awestruck. "Rattlesnakes."

"They like the shade in there. No idea how many there are, but there's gotta be dozens. When it rains, the water collects in different parts of it sometimes, like that little spot in the dashboard there. Sometimes, if you get far enough away and use binoculars you'll see rabbits going in for a drink and never coming out."

Sunny clasped her hands excitedly. "I totally need to see a snake eat a rabbit," she said.

"Well, I've never seen it actually *happen*," I said. "But I did see a little hare disappear in there once, then it sort of screamed a little, then it never came out."

"It *screamed?*"

"That's the only sound rabbits and hares make," I said. "Right before they die, they make this high-pitched noise, like a busted chew-toy. They scream."

"That's some grim stuff, James," Sunny said. When she spoke it sounded like a purr, with a restrained grin and a creepy glint in her eye. I wasn't sure if I was *attracted* to her or *afraid* of her. Either way, my pulse quickened for a moment.

The sun was too high in the sky to hang

around out there for much longer, so we decided we'd return some other time, maybe after a good rain to see if anything goes into the Buick for a drink of water and gets eaten.

As we hiked back to the Dropouts, Sunny asked me if I was going to try again to buy a soda.

"What do you mean?"

"Yesterday," she said. "You went in to buy a pop and came back without one. Total pop-buying fail."

"Got sidetracked," I said.

"That girl in there, the cute little one with the short blonde hair. I bet she could be pretty distracting for a kid trying to focus on a complex task like buying a bottle of pop." She grinned, teasing.

"Possibly."

"So what's the story there? You got a little crush?"

We'd arrived at the western edge of the Dropouts, and sat in the shade of one of the dozens of solar panels lining the base of the hillside.

"She and I have been friends since we were little kids. Dad moved out here when I was four, and she and I used to play together all summer."

"That's adorable."

"I saved her from a snake once," I said.

"Story, please."

"Not much of a story. We were walking down to the general store from my house, and this little king snake pops out of nowhere, just kind of appears right there at our feet. They're not venomous or anything, I mean they're pretty harmless, but Dayle is totally phobic when it comes to snakes. She just shuts down completely. Loses her mind.

"So she sees this snake in front of us next to the road, and just jumps into my arms, screaming. And this was... I guess four years ago. We were twelve I think. And it's not like I was ever a strong guy, but Dayle's super-tiny so I didn't have much trouble carrying her past the snake. We were almost halfway to the general store before she let me put her down."

"I bet you just *hated* that," Sunny said with a grin.

"I suppose I didn't mind." I couldn't help smiling at the memory. "We used to mail letters to each other while I was back in Boston during the rest of the year. I still have all of them." I thought Sunny was going to be jealous, but instead she seemed genuinely interested.

"Must've sucked, not seeing her for the last few years," she said.

I nodded. "I was really looking forward to... *reconnecting* this summer."

"And she wasn't as excited to reconnect as you were," Sunny said.

"Nope."

Sunny squinted into the sky, her nose

wrinkled and her eyes nearly shut against the bright afternoon. "So either she's pissed at you for something you haven't mentioned yet, or she's got a new guy and doesn't want any complications."

"Bingo," I said.

"Which?"

"She's got a guy. Saw them together yesterday."

"Sorry, dude."

I shrugged. "Whatever. I should be happy that *she's* happy, right? I mean, it's not like we were ever actually in a relationship, I mean not a romantic one, anyway."

"True, but it still sucks."

We stopped at a spigot mounted to a post on the western side of the Dropouts, and Sunny bent low to drink from it. When she finished I did the same, but half the water rolled across my face and ended up on my shirt. The world's most awkward drinking fountain.

Close by, a skinny blonde kid of fourteen or fifteen sat on a rock and took apart the engine from a mini-bike. He laid bolts and gaskets neatly on a rag spread out next to him as he removed each part, wiping it clean with another rag and a quick shot of degreaser.

"I've seen this kid around," Sunny said to me. "Check this out."

She walked over, and while he was focused on a particularly stubborn bolt, she nudged one of the gaskets off the rag and pushed it into the dirt with the toe of her sneaker. Sand clung to the black grease like jimmies on an ice cream cone.

The kid looked up, scowling at Sunny. "Hey, what the fuh-fuh-fuh–"

Sunny burst into laughter. "The kid has a wicked stutter, James. I *love* it."

The boy calmly picked up the dirty gasket and cleaned it again with a spray of degreaser and the rag. "Buh-buh-bitch," he said.

Sunny looked over her shoulder at me, and there was a cruel twinkle in her eye I hadn't seen before. I stayed back where I was and kept my mouth shut.

"What's your name, grease monkey?"

The kid swallowed hard and took a deep breath, his gaze fixed on Sunny. "Luh-luh-luh..." He paused, took another breath and tried again. "Luke."

Sunny grinned. "I'm going to call you Stuttering Luke."

Luke just stared at us, looking tired and bored. He'd clearly been through this plenty of times before, but probably not here in the Dropouts. He should have been safe from this kind of thing here. He fixed his gaze on Sunny as he raised a fist, his middle finger slowly extending upward.

You can't stutter in sign language.

"Now *that* I understand," Sunny cackled, clapping her hands.

"Come on, Sunny, give the kid a break—" I began. She whirled around as though I'd poked her with a spear. She wasn't smiling.

"Shut it, James. This is my fun and it's over when I say it's over."

I lowered my gaze, nodding, but after a moment she sighed loudly, dramatically, stomping her feet in the dust like a child and said, "*Fine.* You sucked all the fun out of it anyway, James." As we walked away she called over her shoulder, "Buh-buh-buh-bye, Luh-luh-Luke."

* * *

An hour later I stood and brushed the dust off my jeans. We'd been sitting in the shade of an empty RV on the east side of the Dropouts, looking for shapes in the few clouds passing overhead. I didn't bring up Stuttering Luke but it still bothered me, the way she had turned so suddenly mean-spirited at the sight of someone in a position of weakness like that. "I should probably get home," I said. "Hardly saw Dad at all since I got here, except for dinners and some TV before bed. Wouldn't kill me to be a decent son and spend some time with him."

Sunny looked up, shielding her eyes from the low sun with her hand. "You gonna walk home or hitch a ride?"

I'd planned to walk, and there was no guarantee that anyone with a truck I could hide in would be headed into town right now anyway. "Walk," I said. "But I was kind of looking forward to the other boob."

Sunny got to her feet and grinned. "Yeah, not today, buddy. Gonna save that bargaining chip for another time."

"Figures."

"Until tomorrow, Jamie."

"James," I corrected her, as I set off on the long walk home.

* * *

The sun had dropped low in the west, and as I climbed the hill to Dad's house I paused to take in the landscape below. The desert seems kind of flat and uniform when you're down in it, but from a little ways up you can see how it rises and falls, how the sand flows and the brush grows dense in some areas and sparse in others. The sunset lit everything I could see in gold and red, the shadows deep and black. At this time of day, the desert looked ominous—like it was some kind of trap, luring you in with its beauty, making you want to walk around down there, but then a hole would open beneath your feet and it would swallow you up before anyone knew you were gone.

It had happened before—people went hiking out there and just never came back. Too many little canyons and holes and places to get lost or trapped.

Hike down along a ravine when a good rain starts to fall and you could drown in the runoff before you even knew the water was coming.

That's how it all worked down there, in the desert. Deception. Snakes, lizards, all kinds of animals—they hunt by laying in wait, they hide and blend into their surroundings and surprise their prey. Their prey tries to blend in too, pretending it's just part of the landscape. Beautiful things are poisonous, and water is found in the most unlikely places. The desert is successful because it can deceive.

Sunny's sudden turn that afternoon, showing her capacity for cruelty for just that brief moment when she teased Stuttering Luke, it made me curious as to what else lurked beneath her skin. I wondered what beautiful poisons her canyons and ravines held, whether I was like her, or if I was the oblivious prey. Because out here, you're either one or the other.

Chapter 8

Dad and I had meatloaf for dinner, which was both good and bad: it was good because I was half-starved by the time I walked all the way home and it's the kind of meal that fills you up fast. It was bad because Dad makes terrible meatloaf. I don't know what he does to it, but there's some element of *wrongness* about it.

Someday I knew I'd have to say something about it, but not tonight. I was exhausted. I'd walked a mile from home to the general store, another mile from there to the Dropouts, then *back* to the general store, then another mile along route 48 from the store to home. I'm a city kid—I do a lot of walking, but desert walking is different than city walking, I can promise you that. There are hills, steep ones. And the sun feels like it's a foot away from the top of your head.

Dinner conversation was the usual parade of awkwardness. Dad asked questions he thought he should ask, ones he pretty much already knew the answer to.

"So what did you do today?" was one.

"Nothing much, just...you know. Hung around."

"Did you get to hang out with Dayle? Or that Sunny girl again?"

I answered his questions, and he chewed silently, visibly struggling to think of another one to ask.

It hadn't always been like that. We used to have a great time when I was younger, cracking each other up and talking all afternoon about movies and books. But it seemed like the closer I got to being an *adult*, the harder it became for him to talk to me like one. It was like my growing older made him uncomfortable, somehow. When he was really at a loss, he'd dig up an old gem from the past, a funny memory that we shared. It was like a canned conversation we could pluck from the pantry and open up when things were too quiet and weird.

Dad smiled at his plate and chuckled. "Every time I make mashed potatoes and gravy, I can't help thinking back on that Thanksgiving you ruined."

I smiled too. "I didn't ruin it, I exposed the *truth* about the first Thanksgiving. It's not my fault if the rest of the family wanted to buy into the lies."

It was actually the last Thanksgiving we'd celebrated together: Mom and Dad and me, along with one grandmother, two grandfathers, an aunt and a single guy from Dad's office he'd felt sorry for. I was eight years old and had just found out that Dad would be moving away, and I wanted to ruin something. I started with the turkey.

"This is all wrong. The Pilgrims didn't eat turkey for the first Thanksgiving," I'd said curtly.

"And what *did* they eat?" Mom asked

wearily.

"Probably venison. No potatoes, no stuffing, gravy, cranberry sauce, none of this stuff. It's a fake holiday."

Dad smiled. "So a forkful of deer meat and that was it?"

"They didn't use forks then. And the Mayflower didn't land on Plymouth Rock, either. All that stuff about the Rock is made up. They didn't even land in Plymouth, they came ashore at Provincetown."

Mom sighed in resignation and folded her napkin with a pained look. "Okay, honey. What else."

"They didn't dress like they do in the history books. They didn't wear black, they didn't have those stupid buckles on their shoes, they didn't wear those tall hats. Fake, fake, fake. It's a fake holiday."

Dad's forehead creased. "But I thought the Puritans wore the black—"

"The Pilgrims weren't Puritans, Dad."

Mom let her head drop in despair, her hopes of one last, carefree holiday officially dashed. Dad grimaced as my grandmother rose from her seat, shaking her head at the sacrilege pouring from her grandson's mouth and disappeared into the living room with a bottle of brandy. The guy from Dad's office shrugged and reached for the gravy boat.

It had felt good, knowing the real stories

behind these traditions, these beliefs most people held so tightly to. It had felt like I was the keeper of a secret reality. I'd felt powerful, and as a kid, that feeling's hard to come by.

"Maybe I did ruin it, a little," I said, carving out a bite of meatloaf. I said it with a touch of pride. Dad laughed.

He was on some tight deadline for his article, so after dinner Dad left me with the dishes and typed away in his office. He gets pretty stressed out when it comes to getting his work done on time, so I didn't bother him. Sat on the couch for the rest of the night and watched an edited-for-TV version of *Jaws*. It definitely loses its *oomph* when you take out all the swears and violence.

Seeing *Jaws* always made me think of Dayle. We used to pretend we were shark hunters, like Quint in the movie, scouring the ocean for man-eating great whites. There was a battered aluminum canoe a short walk east of Dad's house–we'd found it upside-down in the sand hidden behind a mound of scrub. I'd always figured it probably fell off the top of someone's car and it was too damaged at that point to bother keeping, so whoever had owned it left it where it fell, which was probably in front of Mr. Owens' house, and Mr. Owens likely hauled it a good ways off his property and left it in the desert. Easier than bringing it to the dump in Mejias.

So Dayle and I came across this canoe one afternoon (A brass plate riveted to the bow end said *Grumman*) and declared it our own. The trickiest part was turning it over: a rattlesnake lived under there and we couldn't get him out. We tossed stones at the canoe, we stomped around near it— everything short of reaching under there with our bare hands.

Dayle finally came up with the solution: we went back to my dad's house and searched the garage until we found twenty feet of rope, and Dayle grabbed a big S-hook from where it hung from the garage rafters. Dad hung extension cords and his big aluminum ladder from those hooks.

Back at the canoe, we tied the hook to the end of the rope, and for ten minutes took turns tossing it over the canoe, trying to grab the far rail with the hook so we could pull it right side up from a safe distance. I finally managed to get a good throw in after a million tries, and together we pulled until the old boat rolled up toward us and flopped over.

The snake wandered off, but I could tell he wasn't happy to lose his home. I made a note to be extra careful where I stepped when I played out there in the future.

The canoe—the last thing you'd ever expect find in the middle of the desert—became our *Orca*, our shark-hunting boat, and even though the sun heated the aluminum to what felt like glowing red we spent whole afternoons in it, calling out directions to steer us toward some leviathan we chased. *Ten degrees port, captain! Bring it around to starboard! I see a fin dead ahead!* We scrambled to get the barrels and spear guns ready, and lowered ourselves in shark cages for what was sure to be our last dive.

It was in the canoe one afternoon that I told Dayle I loved her.

It was the last time I was out here before Mom and Dad had their fights about custody and visitation rights that kept me in Boston for three years straight. It was about three months after my thirteenth birthday, and Dayle and I had been closer than ever all summer. While we had become too old to play *Jaws*, we still returned to the canoe now and then—as boring as it sounds, in a place like Burnham sitting in an empty canoe in the middle of the desert is actually something to *do*.

The sun had been low in the sky and the aluminum had shed most of its heat, so we sat on the little metal seats without burning our butts. The seats were perfectly spaced for shark hunting, but way too far apart for intimate conversation, so we sat facing each other with five feet of empty canoe between us, and I asked her if she'd miss me when I left to go back to Boston the day after tomorrow.

"Of course I will, you idiot," she'd said. "I'll totally die of boredom."

I thought about this for a minute. "Are you going to miss me because you'll be *bored*, or because you'll actually *miss* me?"

Dayle shrugged and admitted that, just maybe, she would be sad to see me go because she had managed to get herself attached to me, if only a little bit.

I cleared my throat with an *ahem*, testing my voice, and knew immediately that I was going to sound nervous. My throat was dry and the *ahem* sounded nothing like I expected it to. Who knows what would come out when I opened my mouth to speak.

"I'm going to miss you too," I said. My voice cracked a little, but it wasn't as bad as I'd thought. "I guess I've gotten attached too, a little bit."

Dayle smiled, but she also looked away, which I wasn't sure how to read. "So...you'll write this summer?" It was a dumb question; of course she'd write. We always wrote to each other, every year. But I needed something to say to keep the momentum up, and that's what came out.

"Yeah, I'll write. Why wouldn't I?"

"I don't know, just...checking, I guess." I punctuated that gem of a line with a chuckle that made no sense at all. None.

I wiped my sweaty palms on my jeans, hoping Dayle wouldn't see. She did.

"You okay, Jamie?" I must have looked like a mess. My heart was beating like a drum roll and my skin felt cold.

Now or never, James.

"Yeah, I'm...I'm fine. And also, there's one

thing, because I'm going back home the day after tomorrow, and I figured before I left I should say that...I should probably just tell you, you know, that I love you—" I took a much needed breath and finished it with, "Dayle."

I'd been staring at my knees the whole time I spoke, each thread in my jeans standing out from the others in vivid detail as though I were looking through a microscope. Every thread was a slightly different shade of blue from the rest. My senses, all of them, were turned up to ten. I smelled smoke from a backyard grill that must have been a half-mile away. They say that happens in times of trauma or life-threatening emergencies—time slows and you take in every detail.

Looking up cautiously, my heart broke when I saw Dayle's expression. She grimaced, the way a person looks when they've been told a neighbor is dying. It's terrible news, but less terrible for them than for the neighbor. There was an element of pity there.

"Oh Jamie," she sighed. I waited for more, but she just looked at me like I was the dying neighbor.

"I'm sorry," I said, wishing there was some giant cosmic eraser that could undo everything I'd just said. I'd never imagined I could screw up so much in such a short time: less than a minute ago, everything was fine. And now, I could barely look my best friend in the eye.

"Don't apologize," she said. "It's not like you did anything wrong, you were just being honest." She shrugged. "And that's important, isn't it? In a friendship, you have to be honest."

"I guess. Yeah."

"So...I'm glad you said it. I just, I don't exactly feel the same way, Jamie. I'm sorry for that, I wish I did feel the same, I really, *really* do. And maybe someday I will, who knows, right? But right now I just like that we're friends and I like the way everything is, right now."

"We *are* pretty awesome friends," I said. My voice was still cracking and my throat was dry but I was beginning to feel a little better, having at least said what I'd been dying to tell her all summer.

She scooted as far forward as she could and reached across the wide gap between the seats to me, resting her hand on my knee. I still wasn't looking her in the eye if I could help it, and I kept my head down and studied the lines on her knuckles. "You gonna be okay?" she asked.

I nodded and looked up, our eyes meeting, her face closer than I'd expected. Someday I'd kiss that face, I promised myself—but it wouldn't happen that day in the canoe.

Chapter 9

I met Sunny at the general store before noon, slightly relieved to see there was no pickup truck waiting for us to sneak a ride in sitting in the parking lot. It was only a harmless lift a mile down the road, but it still felt like stealing somehow.

The sun was still pretty low and we walked down the long stretch to the Dropouts in what sort of passed for comfort. I still sweated through my shirt and had to rub the dust out of my eyes, but compared to walking the same path later in the afternoon, it was pretty nice. In three hours the temperature would be fifteen degrees higher and the breeze could die completely. Not awesome.

I asked Sunny what was on the agenda for today.

"A quick stop to grab some supplies, then the day is wide open, amigo. Whatever you want to do is cool with me."

"What kind of supplies do we need?"

"You'll see."

In most cases, the phrase *you'll see* implies a little mystery, something that will be revealed to you soon. It's usually a pleasant surprise. *What's for dinner, mom?*

You'll see.

And then, an hour later, *Yay, pizza!*

But with someone like Sunny, *you'll see* could mean anything. It could be like, *What are we doing today, Sunny?*

You'll see.

And then, an hour later, *What are we supposed to do with a dozen rabid wolverines?* Or maybe, *Won't the plutonium give us cancer?* Or, *I'm not comfortable stealing a plane, Sunny.*

I'd just have to wait and see how this one played out. I was a little nervous, to be honest—I'd only known her for three days and so far she'd gotten me to smoke a cigarette, sneak a ride as a stowaway in a stranger's truck, and be a witness as she stole ammo for a slingshot from the general store...the same store she'd stolen the slingshot from. On day four, anything was possible.

As we shuffled past the tents and campers, all temporary means of shelter made permanent with cinderblocks under rusted axles, clotheslines, and flower gardens outside tent flaps, I followed Sunny as she strolled purposefully toward one of the smaller tents. The tent itself was olive, but a couple layers of bright blue plastic tarp had been stretched over it, doubling up protection from the sun and rain and extending outward from the front peak to create what could maybe be called a front porch. A plastic beach chair sat empty in the shade of the tarp.

"This is your tent?" I asked.

Sunny ducked inside, pulling me in after her.

The interior was nice and cool, the atmosphere tinted by the blue tarp. She bent low, studying a footlocker with a heavy steel combination lock on it. Thoughtfully fingering the lock, she glanced around the interior of the tent before returning to the footlocker, her brow knitted.

"This your tent?" I asked again.

"No, this is..." she trailed off as she lifted the trunk with one hand, the weight producing a grunt as she swept her free hand underneath. "Bingo," she said with a grin.

Sunny let the footlocker fall with a thud as she flashed me three twenty-dollar bills, folded in half. "Nobody keeps their cash locked up," she said. "It's always hidden, but never locked up."

I gasped. "Jesus, Sunny. Whose tent is this?"

"Belongs to a little Mexican guy, Carlos I think his name is. Saw him walking down towards *La Cocina* before you showed up at the General Store. He won't be back anytime soon. Hangs out there for a few hours around lunchtime, pretty much every day."

Sunny pulled the flap open just enough to scan left and right for anyone who might see us, then stepped out into the sunshine as though she owned the whole village. "Walk like you belong here," she whispered, "and nobody'll give you a second thought."

That may have been true for her, since she lived in the Dropouts. But me, I was an outsider, and I knew damned well that around here a stranger stands out like an iceberg in a meadow. I tried to will myself invisible.

I turned to ask Sunny where we were going, and found that she'd already disappeared. In her place stood an ox of a woman, muscled arms folded across her chest, dusty overalls over a pale yellow tee shirt. A wide straw hat cast most of her face in shadow. "You belong here, son?" Her voice was hoarse, stern.

I swallowed, my throat dry. "Yeah, I'm just—"

The woman shook her head. "You're just *what?* Snoopin' is what you're doing."

I glanced around for Sunny but didn't see her anywhere.

"Snoopin'," The woman repeated.

I nodded, wringing my hands.

"You know who I am, yes?"

"Yes." Everyone knew who Mother Gwen was, whether you lived in the Dropouts or not.

"And you know Mother Gwen—" she jerked her thumb at her chest— "you know Gwen takes care of all her children here in the Dropouts. I look after this place."

"Yes ma'am."

She bent towards me, and I could see every wrinkle in her face bursting outward from the corners of her eyes like rays from the sun, every crease around her mouth. Little flecks of glitter in her irises that made her eyes shine like they were electric. Her voice softened. "Nobody's really *the boss* here," she said. "But I look out for my people and I don't tolerate townies sneaking around and causing trouble."

"No ma'am. I'm not causing any—a"

"I know trouble when I see it," she said. "Just look at you. You look guilty as a cat with half a canary stickin' out of his mouth."

"Yes ma'am."

She jerked her chin to the east. "Get. And I don't want to see you here again."

I slinked down the path toward the desert, passing tent after tent until finally spotting Sunny sitting cross-legged in the shade of a camper. "Way to ditch me," I said.

Sunny smirked. "I live here," she said. "You can afford to piss off Gwen. I can't."

We slid on our heels down a short embankment to a dry creek bed, the dust rising and following us down. We walked along the creek bed out into the barren flats south of the village, hiking across the flats in silence for ten minutes until we came to the short cliff that lies parallel to Route 48.

We sat in the shade of the rocks.

Sunny played with the stolen money. "We can buy beer," she said.

"We should put it back. I mean, come *on*. We could get in a lot of trouble. We could get arrested, even." I tried to keep my voice steady, but I did a terrible job.

"Nothing will happen, James. I do it all the time. Haven't been caught once."

"That's not the point."

"So what *is* the point then?"

"It's not right, to steal like that. That's probably all the money in the world that guy had, until you took it."

"Oh, get off it. These people come here and swear off the system, say they're dropping out of society and living off the land and all that, but half of them still have bank accounts with social security coming in, or pensions or whatever. They're total hypocrites. If anything, I'm giving them a push toward the ideals they claim to live by."

"*Seriously?*"

"I'm serious, James."

"You just totally tried to justify robbing your neighbors blind by saying it was in their own best interest. Am I right or am I wrong?"

"That's pretty much it, yeah." Sunny smirked, and then started to laugh. "You realize that I'm like, at least seventy-five percent Satan."

"Try a hundred percent." As hard as I resisted, something about her laugh made me laugh a little too. "Okay, maybe ninety-five. But percentage-wise, yes, you're mostly evil."

Her eyes twinkled as she stood and stuffed the cash into her back pocket. "Onward?"

I sighed, shaking my head. "I can totally see it now, I'm going to end up in jail because of you.

There's no doubt in my mind. It's gonna happen."

Sunny nodded. "If you're not risking jail time, you're not having fun. That's what I always say."

"I've never heard you say that."

"Well, no, but I'm saying it now—and going forward, it's my motto."

"Pretty crappy motto," I said.

"And what is *your* motto, James?"

"Stay the hell out of jail."

Sunny laughed. "That's a good one too. I may steal it when I'm old enough to be tried as an adult."

* * *

I had to talk her out of buying beer. Sixty bucks was a lot of money to a couple of kids, and I knew she needed some of it to live off of—so it wasn't too hard to convince her just to buy us a couple of Cokes and put the rest away.

I'm not really a beer person anyway.

We walked back along the main road to the general store, where Sunny gave me a couple bucks for our Cokes and waited outside as I went in and rooted around in the back of the cooler for the two coldest ones.

Outside, the sun was nearly overhead and shade was scarce, but we found a little bit of it and sat against the building, happy to be a little cooler and off our feet.

"So, what's your thing?" Sunny asked me.

"What do you mean?"

"Your thing. What you're into. Hobbies, shit like that."

"Oh. I guess...not really anything. I mean I don't play any sports or anything at school, and when I'm home I pretty much just read."

"So what do you read?"

I tried to think of something cool to be into, like maybe I read manuals for fighter jets or whatever, but instead I just shrugged. "History," I said.

Sunny's head fell against my shoulder and she made exaggerated snoring sounds.

"Come on. History's not so boring," I said.

"You really think so, don't you."

"I do."

"So what do you like about it? You're really gonna need to sell me on this one, James. I'm dubious."

"Well...I guess what I like is that it's kind of *fluid*. Like, you have certain events, certain *facts*, which over time, as the story gets told over and over, it changes. You know? In reality things may have happened a certain specific way but a few years down the road those events get distorted by errors, biases, emotions. History changes depending on who's interpreting it. And to me the fun part is discovering what the truth really is and seeing how twisted up the story has become.

"Like, take Christopher Columbus. Everyone knows he discovered America when he tried to prove the earth was round by sailing west to reach the East Indies, right?"

"Right."

"Wrong. All of that is totally wrong."

"Tell me."

"First of all, it was already accepted, by pretty much everyone, that the earth was round, nobody really doubted that. The ancient Greeks had it figured out a thousand years earlier. And there's also this: he never set foot on North American soil, not once. He landed in the Caribbean, and never went north from there. Also, he didn't actually *discover* anything in the first place, because what they later called the Americas was already inhabited by complex civilizations that had been established for millennia. Saying he discovered this place is like me opening my fridge and *discovering* cheese."

"You really have some strong feelings about this, James."

"I do. And the kicker is that, even after returning to the New World in later voyages, the guy *still* thought he was in some part of Asia."

"And for that we get a day off from school," Sunny said, egging me on.

"Right? It's *madness*."

"Take a breath, professor. You're losing

control a little bit."

I paused to catch my breath. "Napoleon wasn't short, you know."

"No?"

"Nope. His military records have him listed as five foot two, but nobody bothered to take into account that the French foot and the English foot were not always the same. After converting the old French measurement to English, it turns out he was five foot seven. Not all that small for his time."

"His time?"

"People are taller now."

"Ah." Sunny's eyes locked on mine, darting back and forth, studying my left eye, then my right, looking for *something*. I had no idea what. "It's interesting in there, isn't it? In that head of yours."

"I guess sometimes."

"Must be weird to live in there." Sunny slouched lower against the wall, getting comfortable. "Tell me more history, James."

I smiled, not knowing where to begin, but the words tumbled out effortlessly the moment I opened my mouth.

Chapter 10

Dad scrubbed the dishes clean, rinsed them under the faucet, and then handed them to me as I dried them off with the dishtowel. I stacked everything neatly to my right as we went.

He'd been quiet all night, not even making the usual half-forced conversation as we ate our sloppy Joes. I figured he was working through one of his writing assignments in his head. He does that sometimes.

He rinsed a couple of forks and handed them to me. He paused and said, "I'm sorry if it's... you know, if it's weird. Me and you."

"What do you mean?" I knew exactly what he meant, but I didn't know what else to say.

"Well, you know. It's not as easy for us to just hang out and talk like we used to."

He was definitely right about that. "Probably just because I haven't been here in so long," I said. "We'll get the hang of it again. I wouldn't worry about it."

"Part of it, James, is because you're so different now. You're not a little kid anymore. Kids, I can relate to. Kids make sense to me for some reason. But you're pretty much an adult now, and I never figured out how to get along with grownups, really. I mean, I'm one of them, so I should be able to but it doesn't come easy for me."

"I'm kind of the same," I said. "I have a couple of friends back home, but most of the time I'm by myself in my room. At lunch in school I bury myself in textbooks and do my homework so I won't have to look up and make conversation."

Dad grinned. "I guess you got that from me. Sorry to pass it on to you like that. But at least you got your mother's looks, so you didn't get too bad a deal, all in all."

That was true—I did look like my mother, and it's not like Dad was repulsive or anything but if I had to get my looks from one of them, I'd have to go with Mom.

I dried the last of the silverware and folded the dishcloth. "So you never really got any better at being social? You didn't outgrow it?"

"Never did. If anything, it got worse as I got older. I remember in grade school I did okay, I had a lot of friends. Well, not *a lot*, but you know. Enough. Then in middle school I started keeping to myself a little more, and by high school I barely socialized at all."

I'd always assumed I'd start fitting in once I was an adult. This was not good news for me.

"But," he continued, "that's what got your mother interested in me. I was quiet and shy but she saw that as mysterious and soft-spoken. Not like I went out of my way to correct her."

"So you still don't feel comfortable around

other people? Even now that you're grown up?"

Dad snorted and looked around the kitchen. "Why do you think I live alone in the middle of nowhere?"

* * *

The next day, Sunny and I met at the usual time, noon, in the parking lot of the general store. I got there a little early and went inside for a bottle of water and saw Dayle behind the counter.

She sat on a tall stool by the register, watching as the store's owner, a frail-looking man named Neil, mounted a wide-angle security mirror high on the wall at the back of the store. He stood on the top step of a short and ancient stepladder, his head tucked behind the mirror as he reached awkwardly with an adjustable wrench and tightened the last couple bolts. That's how Neil did everything around the store: awkwardly and with an adjustable wrench. He owned the place but always seemed more like a full-time handyman.

"You guys are going high-tech," I said to Dayle.

"Stuff's been missing lately. Never had any problems with shoplifting until last week."

I looked through the open door into the parking lot and saw Sunny coming up the road from the Dropouts. "Any suspects?"

Dayle shook her head. "If there are, nobody's

telling me about it. Probably one of them, though," she said, nodding toward the Dropouts. She stopped me as I turned to leave after paying for the water. "Hey," she said. "Sorry about the other day. I didn't mean to come off so rude, I just...I mean, you caught me by surprise. I didn't really expect to see you again."

I smiled and waved it off. "Don't worry about it, it's fine," I said, even though it *wasn't* fine, but sometimes you have to man up and tell a girl what she wants to hear. "I was just glad you remembered me."

"Of course I'd *remember* you, you idiot. You just caught me off guard. I didn't want you to think that I wasn't happy to see you. I was."

"Honest?"

"Honest."

We hooked our pinkies together and shook on it like we'd done when we were kids.

"So we're okay?" she asked me.

"Yeah, sure. Of course."

Chapter 11

"Keep your arm straight, and sight down it like a rifle," Sunny said. "Try to—"

"I know how to use a slingshot," I said.

"Let's see how well you do, then."

I took aim at the empty soda bottle balanced on the rocks twenty yards away and pulled the ammo back as far as I could, as far as the bands would stretch, then let it go. The polished steel ball disappeared into the desert far beyond the target, and I couldn't even tell if it went wide to the left, the right, or above it.

"Pop-buying, smoking, and hitting things with a slingshot," Sunny said, grinning as she counted each item off on her fingers. "That's three things you suck at." She took the slingshot from me. "My turn."

She loaded a steel ball into the pouch and closed one eye, sighting along her arm, down the length of the bands. She stood like an archer, her back straight, her breathing slow. Without so much as a blink she released the ammo and the empty plastic bottle tumbled from the rocks.

"Holy shit," I said.

"You got that right."

We walked to the rocks and Sunny picked up the bottle, rattling it in front of my face. Her ammo was trapped inside, rolling around in the bottom of the bottle, a single round hole punched neatly in the side. "Sucka," she said.

Hard not to be impressed.

After a little more target-shooting, we walked back toward the Dropouts, the sun high overhead but feeling like it was only feet away. We needed shade, and hiked the half-mile to the solar panels at the edge of the makeshift town. I kept my eye out for Mother Gwen.

It's funny how the temperature can be exactly the same from day to day, and you think you've gotten used to it, but all of a sudden it just hits you: how insanely hot it is. Hot and dry. Dayle had a pool at her place, and as I lay on my back in the cool shade of the solar panel I wondered how I could charm my way into it.

Sunny startled me with an elbow in the ribs. "Did you fall asleep?"

I lifted my head and propped myself up on my elbows. "No," I said instinctively—but then, "I guess for a second, yeah." Somehow I'd managed to doze off.

"Check it out," she said. "Behind the woodpile."

I sat up and followed her gaze to the tall stacks of firewood and saw a kid hunched over behind it, out of view of everyone in the Dropouts but us. He cupped his hand around a cigarette, trying to shelter it from the breeze as the flicked his lighter over and over to no avail.

Sunny pushed the slingshot into my lap. "Hey, it's Stuttering Luke! We should scare the *shit* out of him," she whispered, barely suppressing a laugh.

The woodpile he hid behind wasn't the best place to be, probably home to God knows how many snakes and scorpions. Or bees. Or spiders, or whatever. The kid should know better than to hang around there, but if you need to keep out of sight to sneak a cigarette, that's probably your spot.

"Just put one in the sand by his feet," Sunny said. "He'll shit himself."

That was true. He probably would.

"But if I hit the woodpile—I don't want any snakes or bees getting all riled up."

"Then aim carefully."

Loading a steel pall into the pouch, I straightened my arm, looking down the bands to the ammo between my finger and thumb, then fifty yards away to the dust at the kid's feet.

He still hadn't gotten that smoke lit yet.

I aimed a little extra to the side, making sure I kept well clear of the woodpile. "I'm not really sure about this," I whispered.

"You're never sure about anything fun," Sunny answered. "Now grow a pair and scare that boy."

Pulling the ammo all the way back, I let out a long breath, focused again and felt the pouch slip from between my fingers, the steel ball vanishing instantly.

My gaze was zeroed on the ground by the kid's shoes but I didn't see the ammo land.

"Where'd it go?" I asked Sunny.

I remember listening for the sound of bees or snake rattles and hearing none.

Sunny stiffened. "Shit."

As I lowered the slingshot, I saw the cigarette and lighter fall from the boy's hand into the dust. His face was slack, expressionless, and a rope of blood ran from his right eye.

Actually the blood ran from where his right eye had *been*. There was just a black spot there now, deep red mixing with something clear as it made a beeline for his jaw, then running forward and dripping in broken strings off his chin.

His knees buckled and he fell forward like a rag doll, his face hitting the dirt with a sound I'll never get out of my head.

KF: And you're saying that's exactly how it happened.

JM: Yeah.

KF: Would you say you were, you know, coerced to try to scare the boy with the slingshot, or did you do it of your own free will?

JM: I don't think I was coerced, I mean I didn't have a gun to my head.

MP: Or a slingshot, ha.

KF: Mike, come on.

JM: I didn't want to do it, if that's what you're getting at.

KF: But you did it anyway.

JM: Yeah.

KF: So, if it was just an accident, why not report it to the authorities? Why not come to us, James?

JM: I wanted to, but—I'm getting to that. It's complicated.

KF: Okay. Okay, then before we get into that, let's—we're going to back up a bit. Now this girl Sunny, you said she was older? Older than you by how much?

JM: Um, a year older. She's seventeen.

KF: And did she ever tell you, or indicate with any detail, where she had lived prior to moving into the Dropouts?

JM: She said San Diego. La Mesa.

KF: Which.

JM: Which?

KF: Which place did she say she was from. San Diego or La Mesa.

JM: She said they were pretty much the same place I think. I guess La Mesa?

MP: I would think La Mesa.

KF: And... okay. Now, did she ever talk about any friends she had, or other family that were around maybe? Anyone she was close to?

JM: She didn't say anything about any friends. And... (inaudible)...only family I ever heard about was what she told me about her mom and dad.

KF: The story about the fire.

JM: Yeah.

KF: And you believed the story about her dad and her mom in the fire.

JM: No reason not to believe it.

KF: That's a good point. Let me just clean up my notes here, just give me a second.

JM: Yeah okay.

MP: Hey, is that true about the rabbits?

JM: What about the rabbits.

MP: That they scream. That they only

make a noise when they die.

JM: Yeah, they scream when they die sometimes. When a coyote gets them or something. But they make other noises too. Chirps and grunts and stuff, they make other noises. Whistles.

MP: Oh. So that part wasn't true, what you told Sunny about the rabbits only making that one noise.

JM: No.

MP: Trying to impress the girl with your big old brain, maybe.

JM: You never know what will impress a girl.

KF: Okay, I want to jump ahead now, if that's all right James. The boy, the victim. Luke Pelletier, you say you didn't know him, you weren't friends or anything like that?

JM: No, I never saw him before.

KF: You're saying the first time you laid eyes on him was when you and this girl Sunny saw him by the dropouts, when he was working on that little motorcycle.

JM: That's what I'm saying.

(Inaudible)

KF: Not even around town, or in the general store? Or, what was that place, Mike, with the carne asada?

MP: La Cocina.

KF: You never saw him anywhere before?

JM: He was a Dropouts kid. There are lots of Dropouts people I've never seen before.

KF: Okay. Okay, I'm going to want to revisit that, James. We'll come back to that part about Luke Pelletier in a little while, if that's all right.

Chapter 12

I dropped to my hands and knees, retching in the dust. I couldn't feel anything at all–it was like I was floating inside of myself, the connection between my mind and body severed as I watched my breakfast hit the ground like it was a movie. The lifeless body of a stranger very close to my age sprawled in the background, out of focus.

I felt like maybe I could hide inside myself, just stop watching the movie, turn away and find a dark corner way back on the inside and not have to think about what had just happened.

What I had just done.

The movie showed me retching again.

Out of the fuzzy background came Sunny's voice: vague, echoed murmurs. I turned my head and tried to focus on what she was saying.

"Are you listening to me, James?"

I nodded. Beyond Sunny's feet, half a football field away, the boy lay in the dirt, the dust already settling. It powdered his hair and his clothes, blending the colors of his skin and his shirt with the desert palette. The dust collected the most nearest the ground, blurring the line where the desert ended and the boy's body began.

"What did I just say?"

"Huh?"

She crouched next to me, pulling my chin upward with one hand until I was forced to watch her lips as she spoke. "This never happened, James. We were never even here, were we?"

"Yes."

"Yes we weren't here or yes we *were* here?"

"Uh huh."

She crouched even lower and pulled my head back by my hair, as far back as it would go until I couldn't swallow and it was hard to breathe.

"It's important that you understand this, James. You can't speak a word of what happened here today. You and me, we were out by the Buick screwing around with the rattlesnakes."

She gave my hair a jerk. "Right, James?"

"Right."

"Where were we today?"

"Buick. Snakes."

She let me go and I flopped onto my back, staring straight upwards into the sky. This couldn't be real. Sunny stood and kicked my shoulder, hard. "We need something to dig a hole with," she said.

"You want to bury him?"

"No, we need to bury your puke." She pointed at the mess I'd left in the sand. "That's evidence, James, and so is the slingshot, the bag of ammo, our footprints in the dirt here...we have to get rid of it all. Can I count on your help, or are you going to sit and whimper there like a Sally all afternoon?"

I looked around, then got to my feet when I saw a wide piece of plastic that had broken off the underside of one of the solar panels. I picked it up. "This might work as a shovel."

Sunny snatched it from my hand and dug a hole in the dirt about a foot deep, a foot around, and pushed my breakfast into the bottom. She filled it in, carefully scattering loose sand and a few blades of dead grass over the top so it matched the area around it.

She did the same with where we'd been sitting, getting low to the ground, searching for footprints or handprints in the dust, anything that could possibly could lead to us having been there. She swept away each clue with her palm, tossing a layer of sand and dust over where we'd been as we backed away onto the hard-packed path that encircled the Dropouts.

When she was satisfied with her work, we cautiously—but not suspiciously—worked our way around the little village's border, keeping ourselves out of sight behind trailers, woodpiles, whatever could shield us from the view of anyone who might be around. If we were spotted, hopefully we wouldn't look like we were hiding, but the point was not to be seen in the first place.

When we arrived at the eastern side, by the road that led out of the valley to the general store, Sunny and I sat down in the shade of a Joshua tree while she figured out our next move.

"I'm not sure there's any way to get you home without just walking down that road in plain sight, James."

"Okay." I still felt like I was floating outside of myself, totally disconnected from everything that was happening, which was fine with me—I didn't really want to be too connected right then anyway.

"You're not paying attention, James. It's not okay. You can't just walk out of here right after that boy's been killed and have everybody see you. You don't live here, you have no reason to be here, and I doubt anybody in the Dropouts will remember ever having seen you before. Strangers aren't forgotten around here. Believe me, they'll notice you."

Of course, she was right. She was always right.

We sat for a few minutes, hoping a new option to get me back home unseen would present itself, and eventually it did. A vehicle hummed along the narrow road into the valley, and I recognized it as a delivery truck from the Ace hardware store in Mejias. Probably bringing in those little propane bottles people use to run camp stoves or new screens for somebody's front door. That hardware store did a lot of business out here.

"Well, there's your ride, James."

We scrambled out of sight as the truck came nearer, the dust it kicked up staying low and close behind it, so we didn't see until it had rumbled past that it towed a trailer behind it.

The trailer was a low, open type, with a tarp stretched over what was probably a couple of lawnmowers. I knew exactly what end of town he'd be headed to, if he hadn't already been there—only a few families in Burnham bothered to maintain an actual lawn, and they were all clustered together on the hill near my dad's house.

The truck stopped close to us and the driver hopped out, carrying a box to the door of an RV set back a little ways from the road. Sunny put a hand on my shoulder. "Looks like you got lucky. All aboard, James."

She led me to the trailer, mostly obscured by the backside of another RV, and lifted the tarp as I crawled under.

"What did you do today?" she asked me.

"I went to the Buick with Sunny and we messed around with the snakes."

"Do anything else?"

I shook my head.

After a couple of minutes the driver jumped back into the truck, the big engine roaring and pumping exhaust under my tarp. I coughed, but doubted that anyone heard me.

I breathed into my shirt, fumes from the truck coming at me from the front and dust from the road coming up from underneath the wire grate that made up the floor of the trailer. The sunlight passing though the royal blue tarp made everything cool and indigo.

As the truck turned off the dirt road from the Dropouts onto Route 48, I was able to breathe easier, though the dust and fumes didn't really bother me like they should've. I still felt like I was in a dream, as clumsy and cliché at it sounds, but it's the only way to put it—I felt as though I could leap out from under the tarp and into the grille of a passing car and, whatever...who cares. Everything would be fine because none of this was real.

I knew where I was by the turns in the road, the way the truck slowed at certain places, the sound of the driver shifting to a lower gear when he came to the hill by my dad's house. I squirmed to the very back of the trailer and when we came to the stop sign at the top of the hill, I slid out into the low afternoon sun.

The truck pulled away after barely coming to a stop, which I figure it wouldn't have if the driver had seen some dirty kid roll out the back, and I should've felt relieved that I'd managed to get so close to home without anyone seeing me, but instead I just wanted to wash the dust off of me and fall asleep for a couple of years. I walked halfway down the hill and up the steps to Dad's house.

Inside, Dad typed away in his office. If he heard me come in, he didn't say anything. I showered and lay on my bed after, air-drying under a ceiling fan, praying for sleep but knowing it wouldn't come for a very long time.

Chapter 13

When Dad called up to me at dinnertime, I said I'd eaten a bunch of junk food in town and wasn't feeling well. I'm probably done for the night, I told him. I'm exhausted and sunburned and queasy and might as well just call it a day.

Okay. Feel better, James.

Good night Dad, I love you.

* * *

I didn't sleep. I stared at the ceiling until three o'clock in the morning when I rolled over and propped myself up on my elbows to look out the window by my bed.

In the starlit distance, westward toward the valley in the span of nothingness where there are no houses or streets I saw tiny lights flickering, little yellow dots like stars or fireflies. They buzzed around each other, jumping from spot to spot.

I realized what I saw were the flashlights of searchers playing over the sand as they combed the empty desert that was probably still warm from the heat of the day before, the last day a boy named Luke tried to sneak a cigarette behind a woodpile in the Dropouts.

And as I watched the tiny lights jump and

twinkle I heard voices coming through the open window, distant and undefined at first, only identifiable as human because I knew they weren't coyotes—although it did kind of sound like far-off howling. Soon there were more of them, some closer than others, some men, some women.

LUKE, they called. *LUUUUUKE.*

I knotted my sheets up in my fists, worried that they would find him, and worried that they wouldn't.

Chapter 14

Morning came and I watched it happen, no stopping it, from the first shades of cobalt in the east to the full rise of the sun in an empty blue sky. The sleep I'd prayed for never arrived, and eventually dad called me down to breakfast.

"How you feeling? Any better?"

I sunk into a chair at the kitchen table, feeling as sick as I was pretending to be. Dad pushed a plate of eggs and toast in front of me and turned back to the stove to cook his own.

"A boy went missing yesterday," he said. "It's all over town. A kid named Luke Pelletier, lives in the Dropouts."

I pushed the eggs around my plate, hid some under the toast. "Jeez. Anybody know what happened?"

"Not that I've heard. I haven't been out since early though, so if anything new developed in the last few hours I wouldn't know. Maybe you should run into town, see if there's any updates."

"Maybe." My eggs were already getting cold but I forced down a couple of bites and changed the subject. "So what do they have you writing now? More financial stuff?"

"Actually, no. I have to write a short biography of Kurt Gödel for a foundation one of his relatives created. They don't want the usual encyclopedia-style copy, so I'm trying to dress the story up a bit."

"I don't think I've heard of him."

"He was a bit of a hero of mine, when I was younger. He was a mathematical genius, a philosopher, as close to a rock star as someone in his field can get, more or less."

"Like Einstein?" I asked.

"Yes and no. Some of their areas of study overlapped. They were great friends, actually. But I'm having trouble with how to handle the end, the part where he dies. I can't leave it out, but—"

"How did he die?"

Dad slid a piece of bread into the toaster. "It was awful. When he got older he began to have *persecutory delusions.* He believed he was being targeted by someone, someone who wanted him dead. He thought this person was trying to poison him."

"Was someone really after him?"

"Oh, no. Hardly. Gödel was mentally ill, but to him this person who wanted him dead was as real as you or me. He refused to eat *anything* unless someone he trusted tasted it for him first. His wife volunteered, just to get him to eat. She was the only person he trusted, towards the end.

"And eventually, his wife became ill and had to be hospitalized. While she was away, Gödel stopped eating altogether for fear of being poisoned. He wouldn't take a bite of anything without her to tell him it was safe, and he went so long without eating that he starved to death."

"Whoa."

"Yeah. It's amazing how powerful a delusion can be. I mean this guy wasted away to nothing, he died from starvation before his mind would even consider the possibility that his version of reality was flawed. Fascinating stuff."

Dad slid a couple of eggs from the pan onto a plate and stared at the toaster for a minute until the bread popped up, not quite toasted. He shrugged and dropped it onto his plate anyway, carrying it off to his little room in the back.

"Deadline's getting close," he said to me from down the hall. "Crunch time. You should get out, get some fresh air. You'll feel better."

I scraped the eggs off into a small bowl and set it outside the back door for Mrs. McCarthy's cat, and the rest went into the trash. Food wasn't going to make me feel any better. I didn't deserve to have someone cook me breakfast, anyway.

Chapter 15

The state police came to Burnham. They didn't usually pass through unless there was a reason, and the reason was rarely anything serious. Burnham has a resident sheriff—a round, doughy, older guy everyone calls Sheriff Pete—but he doesn't do much beyond drive around really slow and get free coffee at the general store.

I saw two cruisers on my way to see Dayle; they passed me on the road headed south, like they might be on their way to the Dropouts. My stomach tightened.

Dayle sat behind the counter when I got to the store, ringing up a case of bottled water. "On my break in ten," she said. "Meet me out back?"

I hung around outside behind the store, sitting on a cinderblock in the shade. It was around ten o'clock, and if Sunny was going to show up it probably wouldn't be until our usual time at noon—at which point I'd already be back home. I didn't really want to see Sunny today.

The back door squealed as it opened, and Dayle scrunched her face up as the morning sun blazed down on her. She came down the steps and pulled up a cinderblock next to me. "Crazy," was all she said after a long stretch of silence.

"They find him yet?" I asked. "Is he okay?"

"This morning. Backside of the Dropouts by the solar panels. Dead. Cops are saying it wasn't an accident." She wiped the back of her hand across her eyes, and I could see they were red and puffy.

"Murder?"

"Everyone's saying he got shot in the head." She drew in a long breath and I saw she was shaking.

"You okay? I mean...did you know the kid? Were you close?"

"He came into the store all the time, we got to know each other pretty well. He was a good guy."

I wiped my wet palms on my jeans. "So do they have, like...are there any suspects?"

"Nothing I've heard about. It's not like he had any enemies, so it was either a totally random murder and we have a psycho on the loose in Burnham, or it was some kind of bizarre hunting accident and somebody playing with a rifle out in the desert made a hell of a mistake."

"I'm sure it wasn't really done on purpose," I said, my throat dry.

"They're not even saying he was shot, but he has a hole in his head I guess, and it sounds like he died pretty much right away." She tucked her hair behind her ear and I saw her nails were painted–she wasn't the tomboy I remembered. "I don't know what else could have happened."

I nodded, afraid to speak. Who *knows* what I might say by accident.

Dayle gazed at her shoes, but her eyes were focused much further way, like she was staring deep down into the center of the earth. "It's just so—" She paused and shuddered. "This kind of thing doesn't *happen* around here. At least it's not supposed to."

"No, I guess it isn't."

Dayle played with her pocketknife, a little Swiss Army knockoff I'd seen her use to open boxed deliveries. She pulled the blade open with her thumbnail and snapped it closed again, over and over. "This kind of thing ever happen in Boston?" She asked.

Depends what you mean, I thought. *Do kids go missing and turn up dead the next day? Sure. Do I walk out of my house and murder a random boy before dinner? Not very often.*

The thought of myself as a murderer caused what little there was in my stomach to rise in my throat, and as I swallowed hard to keep it down I could feel my heart beating in my chest like it was trying to pound its way out. "It happens sometimes," I managed to say.

"It's funny," Dayle said, "how this town lives for news, for anything that's out of the ordinary. Like, someone gets drunk and steps in Mrs. Erikson's flowers and the whole town buzzes over it. But now...we'd all give anything to be able to go back to our normal, boring lives."

It was true. Burnham was virtually powered by gossip. There was a town paper, the *Burnham*

Sun, which came out once a week. I remember once there was a story right on the front page about a half-dozen bikers who passed through town. They rode in from the south, pulled into the general store for beer and snacks, and rode off to the north. The whole town obsessed with theories as to who they were, where they were headed, where they'd come from. What their intentions *really* were. How sinister they looked, in their helmets with tinted visors. Otherworldly.

A car pulled into the parking lot in front of the store, the sound of its tires crunching on the sand and gravel reaching us through the open screen doors on each side of the building. My pulse quickened—every car that passed, every person who looked at me, I was convinced they knew what I'd done.

What Sunny had *made* me do, really.

It was just a matter of time before the next car that pulled up or that person who stared at me for a second too long was the one who could see what I was hiding, could smell the shame and remorse on me like a bloodhound.

Chapter 16

After Dayle went back inside to finish her shift, I sat in the shade of the building for a while, trying to breathe slow and think myself through this nightmare I felt trapped in.

I wouldn't be able to keep what had happened a secret forever, I knew that. I wasn't sure I'd be able to make it through the rest of the day without confessing to someone, to let Luke's parents know what had really happened to their boy. It was the only thing that would make this sick feeling go away.

I'd have to talk to Sunny first. It wouldn't be right to go straight to the cops without giving her some warning, without letting her know what I was doing. I didn't want her to think that I was *blaming* her.

But it occurred to me, for just a moment, that I *could* blame her. I could get this weight off me and maybe not spend forever in jail if I made sure the cops knew just how much Sunny had pressured me to scare that kid with the slingshot.

It was, after all, her idea to do it.

It's not like I'd *wanted* to do it. I'd even told her so, hadn't I? *I'm not really sure about this,* I'd whispered. And she'd replied, *you're never sure about anything fun.*

And was there even any proof that it was me who did it in the first place? I'm sure there are plenty of her fingerprints on that slingshot. Which is probably in her tent right now, unless she'd gotten rid of it already, which...she probably had. It wouldn't be smart to keep something like that around.

I stood, suddenly ashamed, even more so than I'd been when I'd left the house this morning. I couldn't let someone else take the blame, whether they'd pressured me into it or not. I had the choice to say no, and I didn't.

I'd been weak and easily swayed, and now a boy was dead. How could that possibly be on anyone's shoulders but mine?

I walked around the store to the front parking lot and found Sunny there, sitting on one of the picnic tables. She was early, and she was waiting for me.

* * *

"I can't let you do that," she said to me calmly, evenly. "You need to recognize that it's not just your neck you'd be putting on the chopping block if you start talking, James. I'm a part of this too, and I should get equal say."

"Then it's a stalemate."

Sunny rubbed her face with both hands. "We don't want this to get ugly," she said.

"What do you mean?"

"James. I won't let you spill it to the cops. You cannot, you *will* not open your mouth, or terrible things will happen. I promise you." She paused after each word, giving each syllable its full weight, her gaze locked on mine: *"Very...terrible... things."*

I knew what she was getting at but didn't believe it. "What are you saying?"

"James, you're an idiot but you're not brain dead. You know what I'm saying."

"You're threatening me?"

"Yes," she said.

"I can't believe you'd—"

"I told you, I won't let you spill it to the cops. Period. Terrible things will happen."

"You keep saying that."

Sunny slid off the picnic table and stood with her back to me, her hands on her hips. She faced the valley and breathed in deeply—she was taking a moment for reflection, or maybe cementing her resolve.

She turned and faced me, bending a bit at the waist and resting her hands on her thighs, our noses only inches apart. "The second you open your mouth to a cop, or your dad, or *anybody*, you're putting yourself and everyone important to you in danger."

"I don't understand—"

"I have a theory," she said. "I have a theory

this Luke kid is just the first. I think there'll be more."

"More?"

"More victims, more death. I think there's a killer among us here in Burnham and maybe that killer is *you*, James. This was a quiet, perfect little town until you showed up, you know. Maybe you disappear after the cops get a few tips that you were seen out by the solar panels yesterday, and you run off thinking no one will catch you. Maybe during the search for you, your dad takes a fall off that steep trail on the hillside east of the valley, because someone like me thinks she saw something important that he should check out, and he's so wound up over his missing son that he'll follow anyone anywhere for the smallest clue as to what happened. Maybe someone like me gives him just the right nudge at just the right time and down the rocks he goes.

"Maybe your little girlfriend behind the counter inside, maybe she gets snatched up by the very same maniac who murdered Luke. She'd be an easy one I bet—she couldn't weigh more than a hundred and ten pounds, could she? One-fifteen maybe? Either way, she's no match for a determined psychopath on a mission."

Sunny stood up to her full height, which I hadn't fully appreciated before. The girl was *tall*.

"You'd make such a great suspect. I can see the posters now, and the little *We Interrupt This*

Broadcast news flashes about the search for you, the —" She waited for just the right phrase. "The Desert Killer. No. The Desert...Assassin. Yeah, yeah. *The Desert Assassin*." She had a faraway look, and I could tell she was enjoying the monologue.

"And what would confessing get you anyway?" she asked. "What's the point, what's the *goal?* Is it worth risking the lives of your friends and family to let Luke's mom know how her son died? Would that make her hurt any less?

"No, it wouldn't. She'd still be missing a son and experience a terrible pain that would never go away. And you? You'd have that dark cloud off you, you'd have a clear conscience, knowing you did the right thing and told the truth. You might even feel good again someday.

"So do you want to confess so Luke's mom and dad will feel better, or so *you* will feel better? I think you know the answer, James."

I looked up at Sunny, her face lost in the sun and replaced by hot, white streaks of light. It was painful to keep looking, so I lowered my gaze.

"Terrible things, James," she said as she walked away. "Terrible things."

Chapter 17

Dad stood in the shadow of the front porch, gazing intently at the window shutters to the left of the front door. He held a can of wasp and hornet spray in one hand while he scratched his chin with the other, and started when he saw me walk up the drive.

"Hornets again?" I asked. Every summer, it seemed, Dad would have to deal with a nest of hornets that lived behind one of our shutters. They never really bothered either of us, but knowing they were there made him uneasy.

He nodded, hefting the can of spray. "Feeling any better?" he asked.

"I guess." I knew he was hoping for more of an answer but my mind was sort of on other things.

"Doesn't sound like there's been any news about that Dropouts boy since this morning." He murmured, shaking his head. "Hard to make sense of the world sometimes."

I mumbled a quiet *yeah*, hoping to avoid any talk about the boy behind the woodpile. I wanted to go up to my room and be alone but Dad stood in front of the door and made it weird for me to ask him to step out of the way.

"I don't suppose you knew him, did you James? He grew up out there, maybe you saw him around when you used to come here when you were younger?"

I shook my head, but Dad waited for an actual response. "No," I said. "Didn't know him. Still kind of upsetting though, him being close to my age and everything."

"I'm sure it is." Dad turned to me, his head tilted slightly in a gesture of sympathy. "Sorry you came out here for this. I know you were probably hoping for something a little more carefree, something fun this summer. Hiking, swimming with Dayle, that kind of thing."

"Dad, I—"

He looked at me expectantly, and for some reason that's when I saw myself in him for the first time. Physically I look like Mom, but the way Dad stood there with his hand on his hip, squinting at me when the sun crept past the edge of the porch roof—I realized how much like my dad I really was. I wondered if he saw himself in me, too.

"Good luck with the hornets," I said.

"Oh." He relaxed a little, like maybe he'd been anticipating something serious. He studied the label on the spray can. "Thanks, kiddo. The trick is to spray it evenly and steadily and then run like *hell*."

I couldn't help it, I laughed.

* * *

That night, the light from the porch light outside the window fell on my ceiling fan in just such a way as to make long shadows like fingers reaching above me, stretching across the room almost to the far wall. It was like some giant, dark hand was just winding up to swat me.

I pushed the covers down to my waist, suddenly warm, then just as quickly pulled them back up again, having suddenly felt too cold. Cars passed on the street outside my window, unusual for this hour. Burnham at one AM was always silent —you could hear every little howl from the coyotes or rustle of the night breeze through the bushes. But not tonight.

I stared unblinking at the giant shadow-hand hovering overhead, waiting for it to come swinging down and put me out of my misery; to slap, smother, or crush me.

No such luck, James.

Another car passed the house, a State Police cruiser. I could tell by the engine. It was powerful, but not noisy like the big pickup trucks that sometimes went by during the day.

Would Sunny really follow through with her threats? Would she set me up as the intentional murderer of that boy? Would she hurt Dad, hurt Dayle?

Granted, I'd only known her for a week or so but I'm a pretty good judge of character. I figured I would have picked up on that level of crazy if she actually had it in her.

She was probably just as scared and confused as I was.

The car that had passed by, the cruiser—it was probably headed for the general store. The store would usually be closed by eight, but the parking lot had become sort of a headquarters for the State Police and Neil kept the place unlocked and the lights on so the cops could use the restroom and make coffee.

Somebody would be there if I wanted to get a few things off my chest.

I'd done the right thing, I'd told Sunny that I wanted to confess to the accident, I'd given her warning. She'd chosen to respond with threats instead of reason, and if she didn't want to come clean with me, that was up to her.

I couldn't force her to do the right thing.

I swung my legs out from under the covers and grabbed my jeans from the where they hung over the back of the chair next to my bed. It would be a long, dark walk to the general store.

* * *

It was cold. My sneakers crunched along the side of the road, the sand on the pavement scraping and grinding as I walked. I hoped for headlights to appear and slow, a cop car to pull over and ask me what I was doing out so late and save me the walk into town, but nobody passed.

Twenty minutes after leaving Dad's house the lights of the general store parking lot came into view. I shivered, not having thought to wear anything warmer than my hoodie. I kept my hands jammed in my pockets and watched my breath float away in wisps into the night air.

A hundred yards from the parking lot, a voice from the darkest part of the shadows next to the road made me jump like I'd been stung by a wasp.

"James."

I stopped, my heart stuttering before resuming a steady beat easily twice its normal speed. A chill raced through me, though not from the cool night air—this shiver came from inside. "Sunny," I said. "You scared the hell out—"

"Shut up."

I shut up.

"I know better than to give you another chance, but I'm going to do it anyway because it's the easiest thing, the best thing for me, to have you just keep all of this to yourself. The alternative is complicated and I didn't move here to have my life complicated."

"Complicated or not," I said, "the right thing to—"

"I told you to shut up." Sunny took one quick step from the shadows and was suddenly toe to toe with me, her hand coming up under my chin, gripping my face like she was scolding a child. She tilted my chin upward until I looked her in the eye.

"You talk to the cops," she said, "and *I* will talk to the cops. I'll make sure they know the truth, about how you got it in your head to kill that boy, how you practiced with the slingshot you stole from the general store until you could hit a nickel from twenty feet away. How I *begged* you not to do it when you saw him out there by the woodpile—I *begged* him, Officer, but he had this crazy look on his face and he just pushed me away, saying he'd shoot me too. I was too scared to try to stop him. I feared for my life, Officer."

If I hadn't known the truth, I would have believed her right then. She looked scared, genuinely frightened of just being in my presence, like I was about to hit her or something. Oscar-worthy.

"It's not the first time I've seen him take a life, Officer," she continued, making a show of collecting herself. "Earlier today, I'm out taking a walk through town, just a little hike after lunch, and I see him behind his father's house, and he's strangling this cat. A little grey- and black-striped one, behind his house. Just picked it up and choked the life out of it, chucked it under the back steps when he was done. He's sick, Officer, he's not right in the head and you need to stop him, lock him up before he hurts someone else."

A trickle of icy sweat rolled down my back,

sending goose bumps over every inch of me. What was this about the cat? Was she talking about Mrs. McCarthy's cat, the little calico?

I took a slow step back, then another, and Sunny stayed right where she was, her eyes fixed on mine in a way I could only describe as *predatory*. I kept walking backwards and I waited for her to follow, but instead she sunk back into the shadows along the road.

And I ran for home.

KF: Let's talk about this desert assassin story. Now, you said Sunny came up with that, right then? That whole story she said she would use to make you look like some kind of...

MP: Like a whack job.

KF: To make you look guilty, right? That was her plan?

JM: That's what she said. She said if I told the cops what really happened to the Pelletier kid that she'd hurt my dad, hurt Dayle, anyone I was close to. Said she'd come talk to you, said she'd tell you I did it by myself and did it on purpose.

KF: That you'd killed Luke Pelletier on purpose.

JM: Yeah.

KF: And why would you do something like that on purpose?

JM: I wouldn't. I'm telling you what she told me. But the way she said it I thought it would be kind of convincing, not the kind of risk I'd want to take, you know?

KF: You thought we'd believe her story and not yours, is that correct?

JM: Yeah. I mean, she could be really convincing.

MP: Keith, I got to piss.

KF: Yeah, okay. Good time to take five anyway. James, you need a restroom break, a glass of water, anything like that?

JM: I'm fine. Just want to get this over with and get home.

KF: Sure, sure. We'll try to wrap this up as fast as possible, have you on your way.

(The recorder is turned off for an indeterminate time)
###

MP: I'll call Bev, tell her to get steaks for tonight, cook them on the new grill. We'll get beers too.

KF: Sure Mike, sounds good, real good. So let's go back a little bit, I want to know... James, you said after you shot Luke, what did you say happened to the slingshot?

JM: I don't know. I mean, I don't think I said.

KF: You don't know what happened to it?

JM: I don't think so. I don't remember.

KF: You didn't take it with you, didn't take it home after?

JM: No. Maybe Sunny buried it? Buried it with, the... stuff.

MP: Your barf.

JM: Yeah.

KF: Did you see her bury it?

JM: No.

MP: Sure would be handy to have that slingshot. It's good to have all the different, you know, pieces. Hate to have murder weapons missing in a big messy thing like this, makes us feel better when it's tidy, better for helping us make our case here.

JM: Make your case against—

KF: Relax James. Mike gets a little carried away sometimes. We don't doubt your story here at all. Relax.

Chapter 18

Funny how, with all the threats Sunny had made, her whole plan to set me up as some crazed psycho killer, the part that somehow bothered me the most was the thing about the cat. It was such a strange little addition to her story, and she had so pointedly mentioned it.

I made it almost all the way home—I was just at the bottom of the hill by Dad's house when I ran out of breath and slowed to a walk. I knew that Sunny hadn't followed me, but I couldn't keep myself from running anyway. Maybe if I sprinted fast enough I could outrun this whole nightmarish summer.

Before reaching Dad's house I stopped at Mrs. McCarthy's place next door. I halfheartedly called for the cat, but doubted she would've come to me anyway. Belle always spent the night inside.

I was two steps up on my way to slip back into Dad's house when I paused—would it be silly to check under the steps for Belle?

I grabbed a flashlight from the garage, one of those giant black ones that takes a half-dozen D batteries, and circled back around to the rear of the house. On my hands and knees, I pointed the flashlight under the steps and turned it on.

I gasped and jerked backwards, hitting my

head on the underside of one of the steps.

On her side in the dirt lay Belle, her mouth slightly open and showing her bottom teeth, her eyes glazed with a thin film of dust. Her neck was bent at an unnatural angle so that she faced me directly, staring me down until I switched off the flashlight.

I sat on the bottom step, breathing, waiting for my heart to slow.

Sunny had killed a cat. She had killed Mrs. McCarthy's cat just to make a point.

What else would she do to make a point? Or was she done with making points and trying to convince me to keep the whole mess to myself? Next time she'd make sure I was on the hook for not only killing the kid, but also *planning* to do it, isn't that what she'd said? And planning a murder is whole different story than the kid dying in an accident, even if it *was* my fault.

Accidents are accidents. I was sure the police would have to take that into account.

Poor Belle.

I couldn't stay on track with any one thought for more than a second before my mind skipped on to something else. Images of Belle under the steps led to a replay of Luke falling face-down into the dirt, blood running down his cheek and then spreading in the sand, turning into a dark red flower, a daylily, the kind mom had in her gardens back home.

What could I do? All I wanted was a path, something to guide me, or at least an *option* so I could feel like I was choosing something. But as it was, I had no option. I had to sit on the truth, keep it hidden, or Sunny would appear out of the darkness again, and I knew there would be more at stake than the life of a little calico cat.

She'd proved she didn't mind a little blood on her hands. Or a *lot* of blood, for that matter.

I dug around in the garage until I found a garden trowel and a trash bag, then returned to the back porch. I slipped the bag over Belle's body and scooped her into it, then walked a little ways beyond the backyard and into the desert until I found a good spot to bury her.

I folded the bag around her neatly, trying to make it all look as dignified as a dead cat in a plastic garbage bag can. I tucked the corners back, smoothed out the wrinkles, and placed her gently into a grave that was hopefully deep enough to keep the coyotes from finding her.

After I filled the hole in, I patted the dirt down with the back of the trowel. All I could find for a marker was an oblong chunk of sandstone, so I placed it on top.

* * *

That night, I finally slept. Maybe I slept because there was nothing to agonize over, nothing to weigh. There were no decisions to be made.

There was nothing for me to do but let time pass and hope I didn't lose my mind with guilt, or with worry over what would happen if I got caught. Getting caught was a hell of a lot different than confessing. If I confessed, I'd still be human. A flawed human, still a bad guy, but I'd have emotions and a conscience like everyone else.

A jury would like that, wouldn't they?

If I got *caught*, then I was trying to get away with it. I'd be an unfeeling monster, and while my reputation wasn't exactly the first thing on my mind, I did worry about how getting caught would affect my mom and dad.

Mom, she'd cry herself to sleep every night, wondering where she went wrong with me. And Dad would have to move. Like, immediately. No way to keep living any kind of normal life in a town this small when your kid murdered a local boy.

So with no choice but to accept the situation as it was, I slept.

But with the sleep came nightmares.

* * *

President Abraham Lincoln, three days before his assassination, is said to have had quite a nightmare.

In it, he dreamed that he'd awakened in his bed to the sound of distant sobs. Following the sounds, he walked the halls and stairways, and everything was still and silent. Lights were on in every room, but they were all empty.

Eventually he came to the White House's East Room, where he found his family and staff there, gathered together around a corpse in funeral dress. Several soldiers were among the mourners, and when Lincoln asked one of them who had died, the soldier said, "The president. He was killed by an assassin."

Lincoln was quite unnerved by this dream.

It's also said he had recurring visions of his own murder on each of the remaining nights leading up to his assassination by Booth.

He was unnerved by these dreams, too.

Now, Sunny and I sat up on top of that old half-buried Buick with all the rattlesnakes inside. Everything was like it had been when I'd first come out here, light and happy and funny, and we pounded the roof of the car with our feet to make all the rattles go at once.

It made us laugh I guess, all that potential for death just a few feet underneath us, rattling away when we kicked with our heels.

I asked her, in my dream, what had ever happened to the slingshot. I played it up like maybe I wanted to shoot at some bottles or something, but really I wanted to make sure my fingerprints weren't on it. I wanted to wipe it down with my shirt and maybe throw in inside the car with the snakes, where nobody would ever look for it.

But as soon as I asked, she turned into something else, something *evil*. Her eyes went black all over, even the parts that were supposed to be white. Her teeth grew longer, sharper, not like a vampire's but like a crocodile's or shark's.

Suddenly I froze just from her touch, like I'd been doused with ice water, and I shook uncontrollably. She pushed me over onto my back and pinned me with her knees on my shoulders, straddling my chest, on the roof of the Buick.

Before I could even scream, she had her hands on my face, one hand on my lower jaw and one on my upper, and she pulled my mouth open wider than a snake swallowing an egg. I could feel my muscles tearing, ligaments popping, bone snapping as she pulled my jaws wider and wider apart.

She leaned in close, close enough so I could smell her and she smelled like wet dirt, like rotten leaves and clay. She fixed those black eyes on me and whispered, "*Let me inside.*"

Then, she let go of my jaws and put her hands down into my throat, then her arms. She smiled as she tucked her chin down and crawled all the way in, her head, neck, shoulders and whole body slithered and snaked down my throat and I choked.

I woke up coughing like I hadn't taken a breath in days.

I laid awake the rest of the night, afraid to fall sleep again, wondering how well Abraham Lincoln slept on those nights before his last hours on earth, before he went out for an evening of theater with with his wife Mary.

Chapter 19

The next morning, Dad popped his head into my room. I shielded my eyes from the morning sun blazing through my window by draping my arm across my face.

"You awake, kiddo?"

I peered at him sideways with one open eye. "I am."

"I gotta go buy some stamps and put my column in the mail. You want anything from the store?"

"Nah, I'm good thanks."

"Okey doke." He turned to leave but paused and leaned back in. "Want to come along anyway?"

Dad wanted company. It wasn't hard to tell, the way he sort of lingered in the doorway, his eyebrows scrunched up until they almost met high above the bridge of his nose. Almost puppy-like. It felt like something I shouldn't decline. "Yeah, just let me get dressed."

On the way, Dad studied me whenever the road was straight enough to steal a sideways glance. "Are you sleeping okay? You look awful."

"Thanks, dad."

"No, you really do. You have bags under your eyes. I'd even swear you've lost a few pounds since you got here. Everything all right with you?

Anything you want to talk about?"

Oh my God yes.

"It's nothing, Dad."

"You're not...doing drugs, are you?"

"I'm not doing drugs, Dad."

"Would you tell me if you were?"

I grimaced. "Probably not, no. But I promise you, I'm not doing drugs."

Dad nodded to himself, seeming satisfied with my answer but still worried. His eyebrows were drawn together and his lips were pursed.

Dad slowed the car as we came around the last bend before the general store. A state cruiser idled on the shoulder, and two officers had one man in handcuffs bent over the hood of their car, and another man with his hands cuffed behind his back sat on the hot pavement several feet away. I recognized the man on the pavement. "Isn't that what's-his-name, from the garage?"

The man wore sage green Dickies pants and a matching shirt, the sleeves rolled halfway up his biceps. His hands were grey, black grease filling in all the lines and creases, the rest likely stained permanently from decades under the hood. His light blue eyes were striking amid the dirt that seemed to be part of his pigmentation, as though *shop gunk* was his natural color. He sat like a toddler, bent forward with his hands behind his back, his legs splayed straight outward.

"John LaFleur," Dad said. He let the car roll

to a stop next to LaFleur, and Dad rolled his window down and leaned out. The morning heat poured in like magma.

"What's going on, John?"

LaFleur spit at the man bent across the cruiser's hood, the glob not making it past his own ankles. "Dropouts son of a bitch came into my place lookin' to see my tools, actin' like some kinda asshole. Accused me of killing that boy with I don't know what. Tore up my shop lookin' for pellet guns or whatever." He spit again. "Fucker."

Dad gritted his teeth and rolled his window up, stepping on the gas before the police could tell him to move on. "I don't like this," he said quietly.

* * *

Dayle sat behind the counter when we got to the store, up on her tall stool, flipping through a magazine. "Hey James."

"Hey." I hung out by the counter while Dad went to the Post Office next door. It was actually just the front room of Phil Parson's house, but it had a flag out front and was completely official. There was a little wooden plaque on the wall inside with the Postmaster General's name on it and everything.

"You look like hell," Dayle said. She squinted at me, concerned.

"So I hear. I'm fine, I'm just having a little trouble sleeping lately, that's all."

She frowned and closed her magazine. It was one of those gossip rags about which actor was seen at the beach with whom, who looks pregnant, who got screwed the worst in this week's big divorce. I never understood how any of that was relevant to real life, but then I spent half my time with my face in history books, and I suppose you could say the past is dead and the present is what really matters.

Actually, Dayle had said exactly that to me during the last summer I'd been in Burnham. I was thirteen years old and acting superior, because she couldn't believe I didn't watch *Moonlighting* and I'd told her I liked to spend my time with important things, real-world things like books about Japanese internment camps during World War II and trips to the National Archives Museum in Washington, D.C. to see the Declaration of Independence.

"How is the Declaration of Independence more 'real world' than *Moonlighting?*" she'd asked.

I stuttered a little at first because I didn't know where to start. "Oh, I don't know—because it's only the most *important document in the history of the United States*, maybe."

"But it's like two hundred years old."

"Two hundred and ten," I corrected her. "And its age doesn't make it any less relevant."

"That's a nice word," she conceded. "Relevant."

"Thank you."

"But it's just a thing, a piece of paper that was written on two hundred *and ten* years ago, by people who are dead now. It'll never change, it'll only be what it is right now, behind glass in the National Archives. It's part of the past, it's dead. It's a dead *thing*."

Sometimes I forgot how good Dayle could be in an argument. "Yeah, well—"

She smirked. "Well *what*?"

"It's not like *Moonlighting* is exactly changing the world."

"We're not talking about changing the world. We're talking about being part of the present, interacting with what's happening right *now*. And *Moonlighting* is a growing, living thing. Every week there's a new episode, and that episode affects what will happen in future episodes. The show *evolves*. It's alive. The *past* is dead, Jamie."

I sighed. Dayle had won the round. "Whatever. Eventually the show will be over and we won't have to see either of those people ever again."

"You mean Cybil Shepherd and Bruce Willis."

"Yeah. Them."

Dayle hadn't argued with me often, she'd just let me believe I was right about everything because that's what had always been easiest. But every now and then she'd let me know that when it came down to it, she was not one to mess with.

Dayle tucked the magazine under the counter and stared at her watch. "Ten more minutes and I'm off," she said. "Neil had me come in at like... *dawn* to make coffee for the cops out front and take an early delivery. Has to be the first day in forever that I get to leave before noon."

While all I had planned to do that day was lie in bed and pray for the end of the world, it occurred to me that spending a little time with someone other than my father might do me some good. I wasn't going to feel any better hanging around inside by myself, and the more I hung around with Dad, the more he'd just think I'm on drugs.

And I sure as hell wasn't going to go looking for Sunny.

"Any interest in hanging out today?" I asked.

"Sure, if you don't mind a quick trip to the Dropouts first. They're having the memorial for Luke today."

"Oh. Yeah, I suppose it would be the decent thing to do, right? I feel like maybe I should dress better than this." I tugged at my dusty tee shirt and jeans.

"I wouldn't worry," Dayle said. "You'll probably be the sharpest-dressed guy there."

Chapter 20

The mile-long hike down into the Dropouts was the most effortless mile to walk. It eased gently downhill, following exactly the same path Raymond and Gwen's station wagon had eighteen years ago when they'd run out of gas and coasted off the road and into the scrub. It was the walk back *out* that sucked.

It wasn't hard to find the memorial service—a crowd of sixty or so stood away from the main cluster of makeshift homes and gathered on a small rise just a short walk from the Dropouts' northern edge. The scent of wood smoke touched our noses, the breeze carrying it away from the smoldering mesquite branches each person held, the ends glowing faintly orange.

As far as I could tell, Dayle and I were the only people from Burnham there. The rest was an assortment of hippies and runaways, young and old —though mostly old. There were a few children running wild at the edge of the gathering, chasing each other with their glowing branches, but the population was mostly represented by men and women in their fifties or sixties. A few looked us up and down, and I definitely felt like the outsider—at least Dayle was born and raised in Burnham. But if anyone had a problem with me being there, they kept it to themselves.

A raspy voice rose from the far side of the crowd and everyone turned to face it. It was a woman's voice, though it wasn't soft and feminine like Dayle's or my mother's. This voice had a ragged edge to it, gruff and hoarse from years of living outside in the dust. It was the voice of Mother Gwen.

She stood on the roof of her home: a battered and bleached 1964 Plymouth Valiant station wagon. Sometime very long ago, the car had been blue and parked right where it had come to a stop in 1971. But now it was baked by the sun and sandblasted into a soft, inconsistent hue, like a washed-out aqua, and years ago had been moved to the northern edge of the village as a kind of memorial to the few who had passed on since joining the Dropouts community. It was where everyone gathered for big news or events, the closest thing they had to a town hall.

Mother Gwen stood up straight with her hands on her hips, and for a moment I felt that rush I get when I'm close to a piece of history; once a visitor to my school brought in an ancient roman coin and we passed it around, taking turns holding it in our hands, and I was so excited to be touching something that may have been spent in the Forum on wine or entertainment that I nearly burst.

Seeing Gwen had the same effect on me. She stood like a monument, like General Patton addressing the troops. The way she carried herself was *presidential*, though the way she was dressed was anything but. She wore overalls and a wide, floppy hat, her craggy face peering out from under the brim through squinty eyes like pinholes. She held her hands behind her and gently nodded her head, signaling the crowd for silence, which they granted her immediately.

"It's a damned shame we have to be here today, on this beautiful day under this beautiful blue sky. Under God. You know *He* ain't excited to have to be here either, at a memorial for a boy barely fifteen years old, a good boy, a kind boy. But He's here, I know He is, He's here when He has other things to do, just like you and me. So I'd like to thank Him for showing up, it was nice of you to come, God. You have a lot on your plate but always make time for the little folks like us and for that we're grateful. We're not exactly a religious bunch, but we are grateful.

"I knew Luke Pelletier well. He was a friend. I remember the day he arrived here with his mother, just a hair older than three. He was a good boy from the first minute I knew him and he was a good boy for all the minutes after that. He always brought me those tomatoes his mother grew, the Roma ones. I know they're not everybody's favorite for just eating raw but I liked 'em that way and Luke slipped me a few on his way to go sell the rest of them for his mother."

Gwen bowed slightly, clearing her throat. "I don't want to spend the day up here preaching and eulogizing, so I'll tell my story quick and make room for the rest of you."

She held the smoking end of her mesquite branch at eye level, studying it. She blew on it to keep the ember glowing.

"You know, we started holding these sticks at times like this because candles seemed appropriate but we just never had enough candles for everyone. But I think the branch is better than a candle, because it reminds us that no matter how solid we feel, how real we think we are, we're just passing through, from one state to another. I don't mean states like Delaware or Florida; I mean right now we're human beings and soon enough we'll all be dust, and pieces of bone. Like this branch is turning into smoke and ashes, right here in front of our eyes. It feels real and solid right now, but soon enough it'll all just blow away.

"We're all on our way to turning into something else, to turning into whatever we become when we're done being people. Angels, ghosts, compost, whatever you choose to believe. I like to think we move on in some way or another. Our spirits, I mean. And I like to think that Luke Pelletier has moved on to some place where he finds as much love as he was given by all of you here in the Dropouts.

"Anyway, my story. I know you all have one

to share, so I'll keep it short." Mother Gwen removed her hat and clutched it with both hands, absently rolling it up like a newspaper. Her silver hair, tied back in a ponytail, fluttered in the breeze.

"About a week after Raymond had passed—so this was 1979, and Luke would only have been five then—I was working in the garden, staking some tomatoes that sprung up about a foot overnight. There were maybe two dozen plants I had to stake, and I was working away, driving the stakes in and tying the plants up. My mind wandered off like it always does when I'm in the garden, but that morning it wandered back to when Raymond and I were young, and I mean when we were kids, you know. Teenagers. Back then we talked like we had all the time in the world to be together, and it never occurred to us that maybe one day one of us would have to go on without the other.

"Well, before I knew it was bawling. I just missed him so much, and I was lost and didn't know how to be apart from him. I was terrified, is what I was. And as I sat there in the dirt between tomato plants, tears turning into mud, carrying on like a little baby, along comes tiny Luke.

"He knelt down next to me, real gentle, and put his little arm around me, and let his head fall onto my shoulder. He didn't say a word, just knelt there in the garden with me until I'd cried myself out, and then he stood up and walked off back to his mother.

"That's the kind of boy Luke was. He was a gentle boy, sensitive to others and so full of love it overflowed him and ran like a river through this little village. I will miss him terribly."

Mother Gwen wiped a tear away with the inside of her wrist and put her hat back on. "I'll step down and let you all share your stories. Thank you for being here and God bless."

I wiped away a couple tears of my own. Dayle's face was streaked with them.

As Gwen descended the hood of the Plymouth and joined the crowd, a kid a little younger than me took her place. Someone near me said, "Poor Kenny. He and Luke...they were inseparable."

The boy, Kenny, jammed his hands in his pockets and cleared his throat with a cough. "Last spring Luke and me was lighting our farts behind the mulch pile, it was real late at night so you could see the flame good in the dark and by accident one of my shoelaces caught on fire and Luke threw some mulch on my shoe and put the flame out. He was real good under pressure like that, you could always count on him to know what to do if there was trouble like when we were collecting scorpions in a bucket and I thought one of 'em crawled up my pant leg peemwise but he told me to calm down 'cause it was just a thing of dried grass blew up there."

At this, Kenny burst into tears and was eventually led off the roof of the Plymouth by his mother.

Dayle and I stayed for a few more stories, but the more testimonials I heard about what an amazing kid Luke Pelletier was, the more I just wanted to crawl into a hole in the ground and die.

Chapter 21

Walking back up the trail to the main road, I asked Dayle what we should do with the rest of our day.

She shrugged. "We can head over to my place...if you don't mind spending the afternoon in my *awesome new pool*."

My last summer here, I'd spent almost every day in Dayle's pool, one of those above-ground ones that was only five feet deep. It was still great, I mean you're in the desert and it's a thousand degrees out and it's a *pool*, but her mom and dad were always talking about getting something bigger, more permanent.

"Tell me about this pool," I said, our spirits rising with every step towards the main road.

"In-ground. Diving board. Nine feet in the deep end."

"Excellent. Restrictions?"

"No glass in the pool area, please. No diving except in designated areas beyond the shallow end." She said all this like a flight attendant reviewing the safety procedures before takeoff. "Please refrain from running on the pool deck as surfaces may become slippery when wet. Urinating in the pool will result in permanent loss of aquatic privileges as well as immediate castration."

"You said *castration*."

"Immediate castration," she repeated.

I smiled, realizing it had been a couple of days since I'd done so without faking it. "You got funnier," I said.

Dayle shook her head. "Nah. Your standards just got lower."

* * *

By the time we got to Dayle's, I would've jumped into a shark tank. It was only a half-mile from the store to her house south of town, but the walk was dry and dusty, and of course, it was a thousand degrees outside.

Dad had driven me home to grab a bathing suit and towel, and then had run me back up to the store. I realized halfway into the walk with Dayle that I should've asked Dad for a lift for that last half-mile down Route 48.

Dayle ran inside to change and I hung my clothes and towel on one of the corner posts of the fence that enclosed the pool and hid it from view from the street. I waited, sitting on the edge with my legs in the water. I could barely resist jumping right in, but I thought it impolite not to wait for Dayle.

A few summers ago, I wouldn't have waited. I wouldn't have even told her I was on my way over, I would have just showed up and jumped in. She'd have known I was there by the sound of the splash.

Dayle trotted out from the back door onto the pool deck, (which had turned out great—it was some kind of fake stone that didn't get burning hot in the sun) and stepped right past me, diving in without the slightest pause. I caught a quick look at her in her bright green bikini before she launched into the water, and I regretted not having the power to pause time. The brief glimpse I'd caught had been pretty outstanding.

She surfaced and wiped the water off her face, pushing her hair back and out of her eyes. "Come on in," she said.

"Where are your parents?" I asked.

"Both at work, not home until five-thirty."

I slid off the side and into the water, the sudden change in temperature almost causing me to gasp; whatever heat the water had absorbed from the sun the day before it had lost during the chill of the night, and even though I'd had my feet dangling in it for the last few minutes I hadn't really been prepared for how cool it actually was.

Dayle was laughing when I popped up, blinking the chlorine out of my eyes. "It's a little chilly some mornings," she said. "By three o'clock it'll be like bathwater though, you'll see."

What I got from that exchange was that I would be staying until at least three o'clock. Nice.

We didn't talk much at first, just floated lazily, enjoying the break from the heat. After a while Dayle asked if I was thirsty, and I said I was.

She ran inside and came back out with two bottles of water, tossing mine to me, which I didn't catch and had to dive for. It didn't really sink but it didn't exactly float either. And a clear plastic bottle of water is pretty much invisible in a pool. I felt like an idiot, having to come up for breaths then going back under to look for my water.

Looking for *water* in a *pool*.

Dayle thought it was hilarious, and when I realized her laughter was not at my expense and just at the absurdity of the situation, I found it kind of funny, too.

"So, the other day," I said. "When I first saw you, you were sitting out back with that guy..."

She waited for me to finish, which I was hoping she'd do for me. I sighed.

"So, that guy, is he, like..." I made some lame gesture, like maybe I was trying to mime *boyfriend* or something. "Are you two—"

"You want to know if he was my boyfriend."

"Yes."

"The answer is that it's complicated."

"That's not really an answer," I pointed out.

"Sure it is. And technically, your question wasn't really a question, it was just sort of an awkward mess, with some words."

I nodded, conceding the win as though we were fencing. "True enough. Point goes to Dayle." She hadn't lost her skills when it came to argument.

She swam past me to the edge of the pool,

crossing her arms on the warm stone and resting her head on them, closing her eyes, her shoulders and the back of her neck dark from the sun. "We *were* together, and now we're not," she said simply.

"So he was your boyfriend?"

"Was."

"You guys break up or something?"

"Something."

"You don't want to talk about it, I'm guessing."

"Nope."

It's amazing how uncomfortable a conversation can become when one side of it is suddenly spoken only in single words. "Well," I said, "um—I hope it wasn't, I mean I hope you're okay. I hope it wasn't a *mess*, I guess is what I'm saying."

Dayle opened one eye, and I couldn't tell if she was smiling or not. "Thanks," she said.

I swam up next to her and put my arms up onto the pool deck like she was doing and put my head down. As distant birds tweeted and the sun warmed my shoulders, it occurred to me that I could easily fall asleep like this, and that it had been long enough since I'd had a full night's sleep that I very well might.

"James," Dayle said.

"Yeah."

"Sorry I stopped writing."

"It's fine," I said. It was fine *then*, there in the pool with her right next to me, but the autumn three years ago when she'd stopped writing and didn't respond to my letters, it was not fine at all.

We'd always had our own little ways of doing things, Dayle and I. We never talked on the phone, for one. I knew her number and she knew mine, but if I wanted to see her, I'd just walk to her house. It was a mile and a half away but it never seemed like much of a hardship.

During the rest of the year, when I was home in Boston, we still didn't call each other. We wrote letters and mailed them—once, sometimes twice a month. And then they just stopped. After spending the summer with Dayle I came home to Boston and never received another letter from her again.

I didn't understand; I wrote but she didn't respond. I wrote again, and still heard nothing.

"How come you stopped sending me letters, anyway?" I asked.

Dayle lifted her head and rested her chin on her crossed arms, staring across the surface of the pool deck. "Promise you won't make a big deal of it."

"Sure, whatever. I promise."

She pulled in a deep breath and exhaled slowly. "Two reasons. One, you told me you loved me right before you left and it freaked me out. I thought our relationship was one thing, and to find out it was something completely different all of a sudden, well, it was weird."

I understood, and nodded. "That makes

sense."

"And two," she continued, "I may not have been in love with you, but it still hurt, always waiting for a letter, always waiting for summer to come around so I could see you again. And then eventually it occurred to me that maybe I *did* love you after all, because when you were gone I thought about you too much, all the time on some days, and then I built this relationship up in my mind that never existed, like we were *together*, you know? But we weren't. We were just kids, and I thought I was in love and you thought you were in love. But you can't really know anything about that stuff when you're a kid."

She studied my face closely, like maybe she was looking for signs that she was hurting me, and she'd stop. "Ever since I was a little girl I spent so much more time missing you than I ever spent seeing you. And that sucks, Jamie."

I swallowed hard, my throat suddenly dry. Before I could chicken out, I said it: "I always felt the same, missing you and waiting for letters."

"So you understood why I stopped writing?"

"Yes and no. I never wanted us to stop writing. I wanted to write more."

The conversation had entered territory that always scared me. Dayle put the brakes on it in the nick of time.

"Well, it doesn't matter now, anyway," she said. "We were kids then. I mean, what do you really know about anything when you're so young? I *still* don't know anything about anything."

"I barely know how to to tie my shoes," I offered.

"And you obviously never got the hang of doing your hair."

"I'm afraid to ask."

She laughed as she studied my wet hair. "It's sort of in this not-quite-Mohawk, but sort of like the guy from Flock of Seagulls thing. It's...unique."

"Awesome."

"Don't worry, you look fine."

"I wasn't worried," I said.

"Yeah you were." She was facing me, her cheek resting on her arm, and suddenly we were closer together than I had realized. I couldn't tell if she was squinting from the bright sky or smiling. "You were *so* worried," she said.

"Maybe a little."

At this point I had no idea what I was saying, what I was admitting to, or if it even made any sense at all. I was just talking to keep the moment going, to keep things moving forward, because she had slid a little closer to me—her head still rested on her arms and so did mine, and as we faced each other with the rest of the world sideways our eyes locked and I could see every little sparkle in her iris, every amber dash radiating from the black of her pupil.

A single drop of water inched across her forehead and disappeared into the crook of her elbow. Following its path I became hypnotized, and a truth slipped out: "I've wanted to kiss you since I was eight years old," I said.

"Please don't make this creepy, James." She was smiling. "Neither of us need to be picturing the other as a child right now."

"Roger that," I said.

Roger that? Who says *Roger that?*

"You really shouldn't talk anymore."

I nodded, and she moved another inch closer, our noses almost touching. I'd never looked someone in the eye for so long before, or felt so unashamed doing it.

As she lifted her head and leaned in to kiss me, I made a silent wish that her mom and dad didn't come home early.

* * *

By the time I climbed out of that pool, I looked like a skinny, light blue raisin.

Dayle had a separate changing room for the pool off the back of the house, and I grabbed my clothes from the corner fence post and went inside to change into them. As I pulled my jeans on, I felt something crinkle inside my front pocket; I fished out a folded piece of paper with my fingers, a lined sheet from a small notebook.

I unfolded it and reality came raining back down on me in torrents as I read six words in large, perfectly drawn, capital letters:

YOU TWO ARE SO FUCKING CUTE

KF: James, tell me about your friend Dayle. You two knew each other since back when you were... How old, would you say.

JM: I don't even remember. I guess we were really small, like toddlers, my father knew Dayle's father. How old were we, dad?

DM: You first met Dayle when you were three, I think, at her parents' house.

JM: So, three.

KF: And you would describe your relationship as... how? I mean, were you two romantically involved, would you say, or was it more of just a casual friendship kind of thing?

JM: In-between.

MP: Maybe it was a little one-sided then?

JM: No, I just mean we were friends mostly, but I guess we thought about it as maybe it could be more than that at some point. And there was that last time I was in her pool, so that was definitely more than just a friendly thing at the time.

KF: The time when you kissed.

JM: Yeah.

KF: So you saw your relationship as one that could... one that might turn into something more serious. Is that something you were hoping would happen eventually?

JM: I guess, yeah.

KF: Okay. So when you saw her that first time after you came back to Burnham, behind the general store, and she was sitting with this other guy. How'd you feel about that?

JM: I don't know. It didn't bother me too much.

MP: But it bothered you a little?

JM: I didn't know what to think about it. We hadn't seen each other for... three years by then, so I didn't know what to expect. I figured she probably had a boyfriend or whatever, so it wasn't a huge surprise or anything.

KF: But still, it must have been a disappointment.

JM: I guess. Sure.

KF: Anything else you'd like to add to that?

JM: Not really.

MP: You told us you'd be thorough.

JM: I am, I was. I just...
(Inaudible)

KF: It's understandable that you'd still be upset, or you know, shook up, in light of what happened to Dayle. It's okay if you'd rather talk about something else.

JM: I'd rather talk about something else.

KF: But we'll have to come back to this at a later time, okay?

Chapter 22

She hadn't signed it, but I knew Sunny had left the note. I felt it, without question. My heart pounded as I stepped outside and peeked warily over the top of the fence and into the scrub carpeting the desert. Nobody was there.

For almost two hours, as we'd floated and laughed and laid in the sun and kissed, I'd actually forgotten about Luke, I'd managed to ignore the nightmare my life had become and enjoy myself.

Goose bumps broke out up and down my arms and across my back as I wondered how long Sunny had been watching us.

Long enough to see us make out, apparently.

I unfolded the note again. Was Sunny... jealous? It never seemed like she was into me in that way when we were hanging out, but the note she'd left just looked *angry* somehow.

No, not angry—it wasn't about jealousy. The note looked like it was more of a bold warning, like the letters on a NO TRESPASSING sign—clear, purposefully unambiguous. Sunny's message to me was unmistakable: *I'm watching you.*

Although that wasn't everything the note told me. I realized that if Sunny had seen Dayle and I together, in *that* way, then Dayle would become the first target of Sunny's wrath if she decided I needed some encouragement to keep my mouth shut. Dayle had become my collateral, in a way; my weakness for Sunny to use against me if she needed to.

When she needed to.

"You all right, James? You're looking a little pale again," Dayle said.

I crumpled the note and stuffed it in my pocket. "Yeah, I'm good. Just still a little chilly from the pool I guess."

Dayle had brought out extra towels and as she threw one to me, it unfolded in the air and landed draped over my head, covering me like a statue waiting to be unveiled. Through the terrycloth Dayle giggled and clapped her hands.

* * *

After I got home, I spent the rest of the afternoon in my room, trying to read a book I'd picked up in the airport bookstore about the Yukon gold rush. I'd reach the end of a line and get distracted by my own thoughts, and have to read the line over again before I could move on to the next one. It took me ten minutes just to finish one page, and even then I realized I hadn't really absorbed any of it.

Dinner would be ready in ten or fifteen minutes, and I could already smell garlic coming from the kitchen. Smelled like pasta night, though I wasn't very hungry.

I thought about Dad, how even though he was my father, we weren't actually all that close. He and mom had split when I was too little to remember very much of what it was like having him around all the time, and since then it's just been these visits during the summer. It sounds like a pretty good chunk of time, three straight months, but really, most summers I was barely in the house at all. Dad would be typing away in the back room and Dayle and I would be off looking for trouble or jumping in her pool, or I'd be hiking some of the local trails on my own.

I wondered if I could tell Dad about what's going on. I wondered if I *should*.

He'd get the police involved. He'd have to, he's an adult and he does the right thing, which was fine, I *wanted* to talk to the police. But I didn't feel good having Sunny out there, watching me. If she saw, or even *thought* she saw that I was going to the cops, who knew what she would do to Dayle.

Well, I knew. Not in a *detailed* sense, but I had enough of an idea of what would happen to Dayle if I started talking that I had to rule it out altogether.

There was already one kid dead; I didn't need to make it two.

Or three, assuming Sunny decided I was too much of a liability to have around. Kind of makes sense that she'd want to get rid of me at her first opportunity. If she wasn't planning it already.

I shuddered at the thought of what that girl could do to make me disappear if she really thought it through, really put her mind to it. They wouldn't find my bones for centuries.

There had to be some kind of option, some deal that could be struck. Sunny was clearly insane, but she could be reasonable if she needed to be. What could I offer in exchange for a guarantee of Dayle's safety? And *my* safety?

She wouldn't accept a simple promise, I knew that much. But I also knew that everybody has their price, everybody wants *something*, so maybe there was hope for a compromise. Maybe there was some kind of legal position I could take where I would be able to confess and explain what happened without pointing the finger at anyone else. There had to be something like that.

I suddenly wished I had read some law books instead of all that history.

The alarm clock next to my bed said it was six-thirty, and Dad was clanging away with pots and pans down the hall. If I ate quickly, I could find Sunny before it got dark. I'd head over to the Dropouts—if she was watching me as closely as she wanted me to think she was, I probably wouldn't get much further than the end of my own driveway before she appeared.

Dad called from down the hall, bellowing.

Dinner was ready. *Spaghetti, garlic bread, no veggies. Wash up and come get it.*

The thought of reaching some kind of deal with Sunny brought back a little bit of my appetite, and I managed to eat a good part of the mountain of pasta Dad shoveled onto my plate before bounding out the door.

* * *

Earlier, when I mentioned how the inventor of the guillotine was killed by the very same machine he'd designed—that story's actually not true at all. A doctor named Joseph-Ignace Guillotin sort of put the idea out there that a machine to decapitate criminals might be a more humane alternative to the use of axes or swords, which didn't always do the trick cleanly or quickly. Someone else came up with the design and prototype for the machine itself, but Guillotin's name somehow ended up forever attached to it anyway.

He wasn't happy with having his name associated with this horrible device; as a matter of fact, Guillotin was opposed the death penalty altogether.

And while we're unearthing truths here, it turns out he wasn't even put to death in the machine that bore his name at all, like the story says. He died of natural causes at the age of seventy-five.

Sunny didn't pop out of the shadows at the end of the driveway, and she didn't appear along the roadside as I walked. If she really was watching me, she'd decided not to make herself known.

I pictured her a half-mile away in the desert, lying on her belly on some low rise with a spotting scope and a sniper's rifle, a jug of water and food for three days. Waiting there, with infinite patience, her eye to the scope, following my every move. Watching me through the windows of my bedroom, studying me through the crosshairs as I ate my spaghetti or brushed my teeth.

Maybe I was blowing things a little out of proportion. She was a psychotic teenage girl, not a Navy SEAL.

I reached the road to the Dropouts, the single-lane path that wound westward into the valley, without spotting her anywhere. For a moment I considered turning left into the parking lot of the general store, where two State Police cruisers were parked, and telling my story to the first person with a badge I ran into. But I wasn't sure that I could explain what was going on and have the police reach Dayle to protect her before Sunny got to her first. If she really had her eye on me, she'd probably be watching *very* closely to see which direction I went from here.

I turned right, and started down the road to the Dropouts.

* * *

Ten minutes later I walked straight through the main stretch of the makeshift village, the dusty road branching off into winding paths that led to clusters of tents or RVs. Sunny had never shown me which tent was hers, but I didn't think I'd have trouble finding her if I asked around a little. I was surprised she hadn't made herself known by now, though.

The smell of wood smoke was everywhere, as nearly every other home had logs burning in some kind of fire pit in front of their tent, casting most of the light that illuminated the path through the little village. Here and there an RV had an electric light or two on inside, but the Dropouts were mostly lit with dozens of small campfires.

The mood was somber; the few conversations I heard as I passed each group sitting around their fire pit centered mostly on the loss of their own, the death of the boy Luke—though a few men spoke of the revenge they'd like to take, given the chance. I walked quietly.

I stopped when I reached the northern edge of the camp, where the tiny homes stopped and the wide desert began. Just as I turned to search a new area, I saw Sunny's face briefly illuminated by a gentle flicker of firelight. She was sitting off past the last tent in the cluster, almost in the desert itself, with a small fire beside her. She sat far enough from the fire that the flames didn't allow her to be seen except on rare moments when the fire flared a bit. Still, I recognized her immediately.

She stared, not at me, but at an older man in jeans and blue button-down shirt who stood leaning against his car, a Chevy sedan, scribbling resolutely on a pad of paper.

The man was, I was glad to see, even more conspicuous than I. While I could be singled out right away simply because I didn't live there, this man was obviously from somewhere *else*, somewhere far from here. Somewhere without so much dust, which he constantly brushed from his paper and which had settled on every surface of his car, a car you could sense he used to take pains to keep clean. The dust around here seemed most attracted to cars with glossy new paint and recently applied tire-cleaner, ignoring the old trucks and El Caminos as though they'd paid their dues and had earned a free pass.

But new cars like this one, and out-of-towners with button-down dress shirts, the dust liked to seek them out. Maybe to drive them away, maybe to test them, see what they'll put up with.

The man glanced around, his gaze stopping momentarily at each campfire, seeking something he might have overlooked. He seemed on the verge of abandoning whatever quest had brought him out here, something that could only be related to the recent killing but a search I doubted was in cooperation with the police. The man struck me immediately as un*cop*like; something about the way he carried himself, the clumsy way he unfolded a map of the area and wrestled with it in the night breeze told me he was here on his own business. Turning to his right, his gaze caught mine and he stuffed the map in the open window of his Chevy.

I glanced back to where I'd seen Sunny, and she'd sunk back further away from the fire, now just the faintest silhouette in the darkness. I felt her watching me.

She was in a good position to run if she needed to, I realized, as to her left was a long row of RVs she could duck behind, and to her right was a path leading out into the hills from which a dozen more paths branched. She could disappear in a blink if she wanted to, and go nearly anywhere.

"Hey," the man said, now approaching me, tucking his pen in his shirt pocket. "You got a minute?" He had a full mustache that twitched at the corners of his mouth when he spoke.

I had nowhere to go. I didn't know what this guy's story was or who, if anyone, he worked for— but Sunny appeared wary of him, hiding out there in the dark, and I didn't want her to see me talking to anyone she might think could be the police.

But there was nothing I could do, other than run away into the dark, which I knew wouldn't do me much good—the last time I ran a mile in gym class the coach just shook his head and didn't even bother to tell me my time. This guy looked like he was in decent shape and would probably overtake me in three of four paces.

I stayed where I was, putting a shaking finger to my chest. "Me?"

The man nodded, coming toward me in long strides. I chanced a quick glance over my shoulder but Sunny had disappeared.

"You seen this girl?" He unfolded a sheet of paper and handed it to me, and even in the faint glow of the starlight and distant campfires I could tell who it was, the photo a muddy copy of a copy in black and white.

I hesitated.

"You know her, don't you?" He bent his head low and tilted it to one side, trying to meet my gaze. "When did you see her last?"

I looked quickly out into the desert again, and as the flames of her fire kicked up in the breeze, I could see she was no longer there.

"Kid, I need you to answer me." He took a deep breath. "Please."

I handed the paper back to him. "I don't know, maybe…yesterday? The day before?"

The man nodded, folding the paper and slipping it into his shirt pocket alongside the pen. "No one around here says they've seen her except you."

"Yeah, well, most people don't come here to be found," I said. "They call this place the Dropouts for a reason."

"I kinda figured."

I gestured to the folded picture in the man's pocket. "Sunny in trouble?"

The man knitted his brows, tilting his head again. "Who?"

"Sunny, the girl you're looking for."

"She told you her name was Sunny?"

"Yeah."

The man looked past me, over my shoulder toward the horizon, shaking his head with a weak smile. "New name," he said. "First time I've heard that one."

Unconsciously, I mimicked his expression of confusion. "What do you mean?"

"Come on," he said. "You help me figure out which of these tents is hers and I'll tell you all you want to hear." He cleared his throat. "Probably *more* than you want to hear."

KF: I'd like to talk again about
Sunny, if that's okay.

JM: Sure.

KF: I'm having a hard time with Sunny
as a... I'm not seeing the complete
picture, I don't think. Does that make
sense? I think the more we know about her,
the more blanks we can fill in, then, you
know, it should help us make more sense of
everything, help us, like, visualize it.

JM: Okay.

KF: Great then. So... other than
having come from La Mesa, what else did you
know about her? I mean, you seem to have
spent an awful lot of time together, so—

MP: You get her birthday, her middle
name, anything like that?

JM: She didn't tell me her middle
name or when her birthday was.

KF: What about her physical
description. Describe her to us.

JM: She was tall, like a lot taller
than me.

KF: And you're, what, five—

JM: I'm five-seven. I'd say she was
something like five ten, five-eleven.
Really tall. And... dark hair, sorta.
Reddish-brown.

MP: Auburn.

JM: Huh?

MP: Auburn. Reddish-brown is auburn, when you're talking about hair color, my wife says.

KF: That's true.

MP: My wife's hair is auburn. Beverly's.

JM: Okay, auburn hair, kind of long, past her shoulders. Freckles. Green eyes. Her teeth were like...

KF: Like what?

JM: Like she had too many of them. When she smiled, she smiled really wide, and it was like there were extra teeth in there. Like a shark. Perfect little teeth that just went on and on.

MP: That's weird.

JM: Yeah.

KF: Was she heavy? Skinny?

JM: Not heavy. She wasn't, like, big.

KF: Mr. Madison, have you ever met Sunny?

DM: I don't believe I have, no.

KF: So you're saying you have not met her.

DM: That's right.

KF: Ever seen her, around town maybe?

DM: Not to my knowledge.

KF: Anyone else in town you can think

of, James, anyone who knew her or, you know, she spent time with?

JM: She didn't really interact with anyone if she could help it. She kept to herself. I never saw her hanging out with anyone but me.

KF: And why do you think she chose you as a friend, James, after going out of her way to avoid all these other people?

JM: I don't know. I guess she saw something in me, saw someone she could push around, maybe.

KF: Is that what your relationship with her was, her pushing you around?

JM: No. I mean not all of it. We had fun, actually. In the beginning, we had lots of fun. But a lot of the time she got me do stuff I wouldn't normally do, you know, like normally I'd spend most of the day reading in my room or whatever but once I met Sunny I did stuff like sneak rides in the back of pickup trucks and smoke a cigarette.

KF: She was a bad influence.

JM: Yeah.

KF: Any romantic interest there, you and Sunny?

JM: No.

KF: Was she attractive? Would you say she was, you know, pretty, or—

JM: I guess. I—yeah, she was pretty.

KF: And no romance? A tall attractive girl and a young single guy like yourself out here in the desert with nothing to do all day and you two didn't—you know.

MP: Yeah, right?

JM: No, we never... I mean, I guess she showed me her boob once. Right after we met. But that was—

KF: Just one boob?

JM: Yeah, one.

MP: That's weird, right? Just the one boob?

KF: Well, yeah, I suppose usually it would be the pair or nothing.

JM: That's what I told her.

KF: All right, so... back on track here. Um, this guy you said you saw in the dropouts when you went looking for Sunny, was he one of our detectives, or—

JM: No. He definitely wasn't one of your detectives.

Chapter 23

Finding Sunny's tent was easier than I'd thought—we just looked for the least conspicuous one, the one with no light on inside, the one that called the least attention to itself.

Inside, I recognized a few folded shirts as ones I'd seen her wear. "Yeah, this is her place," I said. I took a seat on the cot along one side of the tent and the man stood hunched in the middle, his head nearly touching the canvas at its highest point. "Ain't exactly Monticello."

The tent was almost tall enough in the center to stand upright in, but the floor wasn't more than five feet by ten—it was certainly one of the smallest tents in the village. The only furniture was the cot, and along the opposite side were three wooden crates, formerly used for shipping oranges, now filled with her clothes and a few belongings: a hairbrush, a toothbrush and toothpaste, an assortment of books. A battery-powered lamp hung from the center of the ceiling by a bungee cord.

Tucked under her mattress we found a little over five hundred dollars in tens and twenties in a black plastic shopping bag. I shuddered to think of what she might have done to get that much cash.

"We'll leave that right where it is," he said. "She'll come back for that money, she'll have to, and

I can use that." He paused to reconsider. "Though, if she has money she'll be mobile, and I need her to stay right where she is. She's close by and it's only a matter of time until I find her, if I can make sure she sticks around."

He gazed at the money in the bag for a minute before tucking it back under the mattress. "Best we leave it for now. She'll have to come back here for it, it's my best shot at finding her."

"So you're like a...private investigator, right? I can tell you're not a cop."

The man chuckled. "No, no. Nothing like that." He sighed, gazing once again at the picture. "I'm her father."

My mouth dropped open.

"We're talking about the same girl, right? Tall, reddish hair?" I asked.

The mad nodded and smiled, though sadly. "Green eyes? Her real name's Rebecca. Rebecca Heath."

He held out his right hand, and I shook it. "Marcus Heath," he said.

"James Madison."

"As in the fifth President?"

"Fourth," I said. "Yeah. We're related, actually. But Sunny told me—Rebecca, I mean, Rebecca said you two were sort of taking time off from each other."

"I'm sure she said something like that. Whatever she's told you, James, don't believe it.

Don't believe a word of it."

"What do you want with her, anyway? What kind of trouble's she in?" I was assuming it couldn't have been anything too serious, but deep in my gut I was prepared to hear the worst.

"What has she told you about her mother, or about me?"

"She said you fell asleep with a drink and a cigarette and the house burned, her mother died in the fire. She came out here to Burnham to clear her head, she told me. She says she blames you for what happened and she's trying not to be so angry so she can come home and get past it all."

"Sounds like she's been reading self-help columns in supermarket magazines," he said. "No, the truth is a very different story."

Mr. Heath clasped his hands together, his elbows on his knees as if he were saying Grace at the dinner table. He lowered his head, gazing at some spot between his shoes. "It's true that there was a fire. It's also true that my wife died in it. And it's true I had a couple of drinks that night. But—"

He paused here, drawing a breath.

"I'd quit smoking fifty-three days before. Gum, the patch, the whole shebang, I hadn't touched a cigarette since eleven-thirty PM on April first, 1988. There hadn't been a pack of smokes in the house for almost two months. Rebecca set that fire."

"Why would she do—"

"Her mother," Mr. Heath began, "had... *secrets*. And Rebecca had secrets, things I never knew about her, things both of them kept from me. Seems my wife was—" he swallowed, trying to build momentum to get through the next few words, "*abusive* towards our daughter. Physically, emotionally. Rebecca never said anything to me about it, I don't know if she didn't trust me or...I mean, I should've protected her, that was my job, but whatever the reason she blamed me too, as I found out after."

"So she blamed you for the fire," I said. "Framed you for it, right?"

"That's the way it all shook out, yeah. I was a pretty obvious candidate for the cause of the fire. For a little while there, even I wasn't convinced I didn't start it by accident. The cops probably sensed that little bit of doubt, mistook it for guilt.

"To make it even worse, the investigators suspect my wife was drugged so she wouldn't wake up when the house burned—that would make it a murder. They couldn't prove it though, there wasn't much left of her to—you know—test for whatever drugs would've been in her system. But it wouldn't surprise me if Rebecca knocked her out with something, put something in her diet coke or whatever."

Mr. Heath paused and winced as if remembering something painful, but I couldn't imagine what could possibly have escaped his memory until now. He seemed to live in the days surrounding the fire, appearing more focused when talking about the things that happened a year ago than when he was engaged in the present.

For the first time since he began the story he turned to me, looking me in the eye. "I was getting pretty deep into the vodka most nights at that point, and I suppose I could blame stress from work and all that, but the reality is I was weak and just gave in to it easy, didn't bother to fight the temptation and I kept dipping into the liquor cabinet. If I'd been sober I might've been able to get to my wife upstairs before the whole place burned, but that night I was in a pretty bad way when I first smelled the smoke.

"One of the investigators said the fire started right behind me, probably from vodka or something similar soaked into the carpet. And I remember smelling cigarette smoke, like just a little whiff of it for a second, then came that awful smell of burning carpet, the couch, fumes from all this stuff that isn't made to burn, you know? It didn't smell like a campfire, that's for sure. Smelled like burning tires or melting plastic. Bitter, acrid. I had just enough sense to get off my chair and crawl out the door."

I shook my head, imagining Sunny as the laughing girl tossing stones at the Buick to set off the rattlesnakes. I'd certainly seen a frightening darkness in her eyes the last couple of times we'd met and I didn't doubt she was capable of anything, but it was still hard to imagine she'd plan, and execute, the murder of her own mother.

"I can't believe Sunny set that fire," I said quietly.

Mr. Heath didn't correct me on using the wrong name. "Well, she did. And before they could even charge me with manslaughter or whatever they had in mind, the cops backed off and started looking at Rebecca. There were parts that didn't make sense. Like the fire starting *behind* my chair instead of next to it or in front of it or *on* it like it would if it happened they way they'd first suspected. And like I said, the way the fire spread through the house, I guess my wife would have woken up and had time to get out but she didn't. Never even turned over, just stayed there under the covers in the same position she always slept. I had no reason to want my wife dead, but after talking with a few of her classmates they suspected Rebecca certainly might have."

He rubbed one eye with the back of his hand, and I couldn't tell if he was wiping away a tear or not. But his voice was softer, a little more uneven as he continued. "So the investigation started to center on Rebecca, like where she was that night in particular, 'cause she'd said she was out all night partying with a friend but the police couldn't even locate this 'friend' in the first place. She could've been made up entirely, for all anybody knew. It certainly wasn't anybody I'd ever heard of."

Mr. Heath sort of spaced out for a minute, his gaze faraway, his shoulders slumped.

"And then?" I asked.

"And then she disappeared. She just never came home one night. *Home* being a ratty motel outside of town, mind you, but even with our differences after the fire she still came through that door every night sometime before midnight and went to bed. But then one night, no Rebecca."

"And you've been looking for her ever since."

He smoothed his mustache with the pad of his thumb. "Well, yes and no. She turned up two days later, dead. Her body washed out of the south end of Kippel's Gorge, this really rough section of the river that ran through town. I got called down to the county Medical Examiner's office and identified her body."

He air in the tent suddenly dropped twenty degrees and goose bumps raced across every inch of my skin. I shivered involuntarily, an icy bead of sweat forming on the back of my neck and rolling down between my shoulder blades.

"Wait. *What?*"

"I identified her body. What was left of it, anyway. She was a mess—she'd ended up in the river somehow, the police suspected she did it on purpose, her being under so much pressure from the investigation and all, and they being almost ready to charge her, really closing in—and her body got run through that gorge downstream. She was so beat up by the rocks and the current, I couldn't barely tell it was her, but they said the height, weight, and hair color matched Rebecca's. I went up to the morgue and identified her by what was left of her clothes and a necklace she always wore. The M.E. said I shouldn't look at her face if I ever wanted to sleep again. I guess there wasn't much of a face there anymore to look at."

I just stared at Mr. Heath, his features becoming less human the longer I gaped, and seeming more like just a collection of random lines and colors. Like when you say a word over and over and it stops having meaning. I stared at his mouth, waiting for the rest of the story to come out.

"Birthmarks?" I asked.

"She had a couple on her back, one on her elbow, but there were a lot of parts where the skin just got rubbed right off against the rocks, so they didn't see any marks worth showing me. They said she probably got caught in a hydraulic, where the water runs over a big rock or something and the current can just circulate and recirculate on and on, and something caught up in there might stay stuck for a pretty long while.

"Pretty soon after her body washed out, they found her suicide note, sort of. There was a nice spot on top of the rocks where they think she jumped into the water, a little clearing where she would've been able to see the moon, she always liked that. It was a place where not many people ever went. They found her goodbye carved into a tree there."

"And it said...?"

Mr. Heath smiled for the first time since starting the story. "Three words, James." He counted them off on his fingers. "Fuck. Off. World."

Chapter 24

"So if Sunny—I mean Rebecca—is dead, then who lives *here?*" I kicked one of the orange crates with my sneaker.

"Rebecca does," Mr. Heath said. "That's the worst part. The girl they pulled out of that river was not my daughter."

"But I thought—"

"Yeah, I did too, for a little while. The cops were convinced it was her, I mean there was *no* doubt who they pulled out of that water. So I believed it too."

"But you're saying it wasn't your daughter."

Mr. Heath rose and paced the tiny area of the tent, studying the items in the little wooden crates and the blankets on the cot. "Someone broke into my room at the motel, and took some money I had stashed in the back of one of the drawers of my dresser. Nothing else was touched, and nobody could've known about that money but Rebecca."

I sat quietly, looking inward now, letting the story settle: Sunny had drugged her mom and set fire to her house, leaving her own mother to die and setting her father up to take the fall for it—unless the plan was for him to burn to death too. She'd faked her own death and disappeared. She'd—

"Wait, then who'd they pull out of the river?"

I asked suddenly.

"Took me a while to figure that out," Mr. Heath said. "The cops would never have believed my theory of what had *really* happened, so I didn't bother trying to get them to look for any missing girls fitting that description. But I think I found a likely match on my own, a girl about Rebecca's age with the same height and build, same hair pretty much, who disappeared about the same time as Rebecca did."

"So she...she murdered a girl, a lookalike, and dressed her up, put her own jewelry on her, threw her in the river..."

Mr. Heath nodded, his head heavy, grave. "It probably went something like that. She always had this...*darkness* in her, like she was missing something, something that keeps most people on the right side of things. She never really acted out as a kid but there was still—" he stopped, unsure of his words. "I never wanted to know what she was capable of. Honestly, some days, the way she would look at me, look at her mother, she frightened me. Even as a little girl."

He shook off a chill and straightened, his graying hair brushing the top of the tent. "So, I've been chasing down clues, slivers of reports of a girl who might be her who was seen here or there, tracking her down for most of the last year. The trail ended right here."

"What will you do when you find her?"

After a long silence he said, "I have no idea, James."

* * *

Far off to the west, lightning cracked and popped like splintering wood. The bolt was razor-edged against the purple-black sky, a crooked jumble of segments touching the earth just long enough to kiss it and disappear.

A storm was moving to the west of Burnham, one of those summer storms that seem to take hours to gather but then suddenly drops a month's worth of rain all at once, with winds that shake the windows and lightning that splits stout little trees in half. Out here, you could watch a storm pass by—thunderheads, lightning and all, and never feel a drop of rain.

When I was in second grade, a thunderstorm rolled through while we were out on the playground at recess and the teachers rushed us back inside before we got soaked. Mr. McHenry was inspired by the thunder and told us about his hero Benjamin Franklin, who discovered electricity by attaching a metal key to a kite and flying it in a storm very much like the one that had put an early end to recess. The lightning was attracted to the key and struck it—and, Mr. McHenry told us, that's how he discovered electricity.

A few years passed before I discovered that

hardly anything our teacher told us that afternoon was true. Franklin *did* fly a silk kite in a storm, but scientists were already pretty familiar with the nature of electricity by that time—it wasn't exactly *undiscovered*. And luckily, Ben's kite never *was* struck by lightning, as he would've been electrocuted and died instantly.

Interestingly, a Russian Physicist named Georg Wilhelm Richmann of St. Petersburg attempted a similar experiment a few months later, hoping to quantify the nature of lightning. *He* did not survive.

* * *

As we stood outside of the tent, about to part ways, I stopped him, my hand on his arm. I swallowed hard, trying to organize my thoughts and figure out how I would explain all that's happened. "Mr. Heath," I said. "Wait."

He turned to me, and as another lightning bolt split the sky to the west I could see where Sunny had gotten her tall stature. I felt small next to him.

"I suppose you've heard about the boy who'd been killed here in the Dropouts a few days ago," I began.

KF: That's a hell of a story.

JM: Yeah.

KF: Mike, let me talk to you for a minute outside.

###
(The recorder is turned off for an indeterminate time)
###

KF: Okay, so... we were talking about your conversation with Sunny's father, you called him Mr. Heath.

JM: Yup.

KF: I guess... I mean, there's just a lot of information here. I don't remember hearing about a suicide washing out of any river nearby, but I guess we wouldn't necessarily hear about every little thing that happens in southern California.

MP: I guess we wouldn't, no.

JM: I'm just telling you what the guy told me.

KF: I would definitely be interested to talk to the boys in La Mesa though, get the background on this. Mike, you have that buddy in arson out that way, yeah? Maybe he could send some stuff over to us, some stuff on that fire.

MP: I could give him a yell.

KF: Great. Okay, so James, in all that stuff Mr. Heath told you, did he happen to mention any details we could use to corroborate his story? Like, I don't know, like any street names, or the Motel he'd stayed at, or—

JM: You don't believe his story?

KF: No, no. It's not a matter of, you know, it's not that we think you're lying or anything, or that Mr. Heath was lying, it's just that pretty much everything about this whole mess is sort of in question right now, and we're still sorting out who's who and what's what, if you know what I mean. So, every little thing we can verify and check off our list of questionables is a huge help to us.

JM: No, I don't remember any details like that. Not any that I can think of right now I mean.

KF: Okay, that's fine. The... you said the name of the part of the river where the body washed out, where they found the girl they thought was Sunny. What was that again?

JM: I think it was—

KF: It should be—I think somewhere here in my notes I have—thanks Mike, that's it. Kippel's Gorge, you told us.

JM: Yeah, okay.

KF: That should be easy enough to verify. So, now I just want to make sure I have all this right, so let's try to put the whole thing in order, like on a timeline, okay? 'Cause there's some pretty heavy-duty stuff went on in La Mesa, it sounds like.

JM: Okay.

KF: Now, first was the fire, right? It all started with that.

JM: Yes.

KF: So, Sunny, she drugs her mother, makes sure her dad is good and drunk, and sets the house on fire using vodka as an accelerant.

JM: That's what Mr. Heath described, basically. That's what he told me.

KF: Okay. So then Sunny disappears, her father moves into a hotel because his house is burned down, and a short time later a girl matching Sunny's description is found in Tippel's Gorge outside of La Mesa.

JM: Kippel's.

KF: Pardon?

JM: You said Tippel's. It's Kippel's, with a K. According to Mr. Heath.

JM: Right. Nice catch. Anyway, the body washes out, they assume it's Sunny, they find a note carved in a tree where she presumably jumped in, all that, it all adds up to some pretty conclusive stuff. Her father even identified her body, you said.

JM: Uh huh.

KF: So, case closed until...

JM: Until Sunny sneaks into her father's motel room and steals money from a hidden spot that only he would know.

KF: Yes. Right. So then he thinks, or he knows I guess, that his daughter is alive, so he looks for reports of a missing girl who could be the one they pulled out of the river. He finds one, you said.

JM: That's what he told me.

KF: And from there, he ended up in the dropouts. How did—I think this is where I kind of lose the thread, if you know what mean. How, or—what brought him to the dropouts? There's a pretty big gap in the story between him finding out his daughter is alive and tracking her all the way to Burnham.

JM: He didn't say. Just said the trail led to the dropouts.

KF: You didn't ask about what led him there, specifically?

JM: I had other stuff on my mind.

KF: Oh—yeah, I suppose that's true.

MP: The dead kid.

JM: Yeah.

KF: So he follows her to the dropouts, you two find her tent, there's some money in there, there was how much? You said four hundred, if I recall.

JM: I said five hundred.

KF: Okay, that's right. Five hundred. Heath leaves it there in the tent, figures she'll come back for it and that'll be his chance to get to her. Then what?

JM: Then everything got out of control.

MD: (laughing) Yeah, no shit.

Chapter 25

The headlights of Mr. Heath's Chevy swept across the dirt road as we rounded the turn up to the General store, illuminating ruts in the path and the dry grass alongside it. After I'd told him the shortest version of what'd happened to Luke Pelletier that I could, he gave me a lift up to the main road, most of the short drive spent in silence.

"When I said I didn't know what I'd do when I found her, I was being honest," Mr. Heath finally said. "But I do know that I won't turn her in to the authorities for starting that fire, and I won't help you pin the killing of that boy on her either."

I slumped in my seat.

"I'm her *father*, James. Maybe I didn't protect her when I could've—should've—but I'm here now and no matter how much damage she's done I won't let anything happen to her that I don't agree to first. And I don't agree to going out of my way to see her put in jail for something that you did."

"But I told you it was an accident, I—"

"You said it yourself, kid. You held that slingshot, you aimed it, you killed that boy. It was you, James—you, and not Rebecca."

He pulled into the general store's parking lot and waited for me to get out. "She doesn't need any more trouble than she has already."

There was finality to his words, and I knew he wouldn't be swayed.

* * *

As I reached the bottom of the hill by Dad's house, I began to see lights, blue and red ones, flashing against neighboring rooftops, making silhouettes out of trees and mailboxes. As I walked closer I saw there were two State Police cruisers in Dad's driveway, and two officers talking to Dad on the front porch.

I paused, readying myself. I'd kept my end of the deal, I hadn't gone to the cops; Sunny couldn't put the blame on me if I'd kept quiet about everything and the cops ended up coming to *me*, right?

Still, I hesitated. I knew I'd feel better after I explained what had happened, I'd have this sickening weight off of me and I'd be able to breathe and cry and someday even feel good about myself. But I'd still be in a hell of a lot of trouble first, and I needed a second to let that sink in before I started back up the hill to Dad's place. I'd definitely be charged with something, even though it was an accident. I mean, I was responsible and I hadn't reported it until now, and I doubted the cops would care about the threats made to me by a teenage girl, no matter how psycho she may be.

Although—and this thought came to me slowly, afraid to be recognized, but I finally grasped it—the police might be interested to find out that a girl who'd drowned herself in a river last year is alive after all, and that she'd killed two people that we know of, and maybe even more since she'd disappeared.

Sunny couldn't hurt my dad or Dayle from a jail cell.

I took my first step toward the house, breathing deeply, anxious, relieved. But before I took my second step, Sunny's voice startled me from the shadow of a telephone pole next to the road.

"What did you tell him?" She asked. Though it was less of a question than a demand. "Tell me what you said to him."

I gasped audibly, and in the silence that followed I heard the faintest *click* of her lips as she smiled. She enjoyed scaring me.

"I told him everything," I said, scraping together as much courage as I could. "He knows about you threatening me into covering up what happened to Luke. And he told me about what really happened to your mom."

I took a breath and tried to steady my voice.

"You're screwed, Sunny. Or *Rebecca*, whatever the hell your name is. Your Dad knows you're in Burnham and pretty soon the cops will know too. I might go to jail for a little while for what we did to that kid in the Dropouts, but you'll be locked up *forever* as a murderer."

She stepped out from behind the telephone pole, the red and blue flashes from the police lights reflecting in her eyes. She dropped her head in what at first appeared to be defeat, then became a gesture of boredom as she drew a little circle in the dirt with the toe of her sneaker.

"When was the last time you saw that little blonde girl, James? The one from the store?"

"Dayle?" I shook my head. "I don't know what Dayle has to do with—"

Sunny took a few steps closer until we were just inches apart, her voice even, patient. "What did I tell you would happen if you opened your fucking mouth to the cops, James?"

I took a step backwards. She kept her hands behind her back as though she were hiding something, although I knew there was nothing there. But the gesture implied that she had some kind of advantage over me, that she knew much more about what was happening here than I ever would.

She took a step forward to offset my hesitant retreat and looked toward my father's house, where now there was one cop talking to my dad on the front steps and another sweeping a flashlight's beam across the ground by the driveway. Maybe he'd dropped his keys in the dark, or maybe he was searching for *clues*.

"Your dad is safe for now, with all that *police presence*," she said. "But they won't always be there, and I'll be ready when they leave. In the mean time, there *is* that girlfriend of yours, what was her name?"

"Where is she?"

"Her name's Dayle, isn't it? She wouldn't tell me her name. Wouldn't tell me much of anything, really—she just whimpered, it was pathetic."

This time it was me who took a step forward. "What did you do to—"

"I almost felt bad for her, but after about five seconds of that obnoxious whimpering I got over it, believe me. She's not a strong person, is she James? Doesn't strike me as the type to really hold up under pressure."

She still stared off at Dad's house, her face glowing blue, then red, then blue. I suddenly needed to sit down.

"You look like you're gonna barf, James."

I felt like I would. How could this happen? How could I be a regular kid, messing around in the desert with a slingshot one minute, when my biggest problem was that I wasn't sure how to tell my father that I wasn't crazy about his meatloaf, and the next minute I was a killer? And now my dad was in danger, and Dayle was...I didn't even know. Kidnapped? Dead?

"What did you do with her?"

"Oh, she's fine, James. When I left her she

was in a safe place. Well—" Sunny paused to reconsider this part. "No, she's actually in a pretty *dangerous* place, but she's safe for now. Until I decide otherwise. So here's the thing: clearly, this whole situation will soon be out of *my* control, whether you keep your mouth shut or not, and I need to be prepared to move on to greener pastures."

She scanned the horizon, left to right. "Actually, the pastures don't even have to be all that green. Any kind of vegetation would be pretty good, really. Honestly I'd be just fine if I never saw the desert again."

I saw her teeth glisten in the shadows when she smiled.

"But my tent, James, my tent has my stuff in it, stuff I need to get gone and stay gone."

"Your money," I managed to say.

"My money. I know that pain in the ass father of mine'll be watching and I can't get in there to grab it, so I'm sending you."

She folded her arms and leaned one shoulder against the telephone pole, tilting her head to one side. "Better you than me, obviously."

I paused, hoping to slow the situation down to a manageable pace, to get it under my control. I metered out my words slowly. "How am I supposed to get in there and grab it without your father seeing me?"

Sunny shrugged. "Not my problem."

"But what happens if he catches me?"

"Then Dale and that Luke kid will have more in common than just growing up in a boring shithole town."

I shook my head, unable to accept that I was really having this conversation. "How do I find you after? Where's Dayle?"

"You'll find us, James. She's in the one safe spot in the middle of a very dangerous place." She backed away, dissolving into the darkness beside the road like she'd never been there at all, just a voice in my head. "See you soon."

And she was gone.

Chapter 26

As I turned around, facing the way I'd come, a flyer caught my eye, tacked to the telephone pole a foot above my head. At the top in heavy, black capital letters it read MISSING, followed by a Xeroxed copy in black and white of what had probably once been a cute picture of a cat, now just a black blob with white half-moons for eyes. Below the photo was a short paragraph of text:

> *BELLE, Female CALICO.*
> *Missing since June 24*
> *Twelve years old.*
> *Last seen in Mrs. McCarthy's yard.*
> *Will respond to offers of food*
> *(esp. turkey or roast beef)*
> *PLEASE see Mrs. McCarthy if*
> *you have seen her.*

It was a reminder and couldn't have been placed more effectively in space or time. Any lingering doubts I may have had about Sunny's capacity to carry out her threats had vanished.

* * *

The Salem witch trials took place in 1692 and into 1693. The area in and around what has become modern-day Salem, Massachusetts was composed of tightly-knit communities that were afraid of *everything*. Crops could fail and people would go broke or go hungry. Smallpox or worse could sweep through a village and take half the population with it. Natives could break treaties, fires could burn homes.

With such fears came a desperate need to believe in an evil that could be defeated, a boogeyman they could point to and go to war with so they'd feel as though they had some control over what happened to them.

For a time, that boogeyman was witchcraft. And when times became hard the blame fell heavily on witches—wherever, whoever they were. And soon paranoia set in: if someone's chicken died in the night, well, there must be a witch among us.

And as it happens, I saw so-and-so's wife singing a song that wasn't in the church hymnal, and let's face it—that's just not right. Must be a witch.

Paranoia quickly became hysteria and within a span of fourteen months, twenty people had been put to death for being witches (Most people think they were burned at the stake, but no one was ever actually burned in the US, at least not as a penalty for witchcraft. Most of them were hanged—burning was a European thing) and another five died in prison. It took no more than a child pointing a finger at an adult she didn't like to get a trial rolling, and the more the accused denied being a witch, the more one had to suppose that denying the charge is *exactly* the kind of thing a witch would do in such a situation so...render judgment and string her up.

Residents lived in fear of accusation, or even of being associated with someone who was accused. A person charged with witchcraft might be offered the possibility of being spared a hanging if she pointed out other people she "knew" to be witches.

One man was righteous enough to take a stand; Giles Corey refused to plead neither guilty nor innocent when he was accused of witchcraft, on the grounds that it was an absurd accusation in the first place and the hysteria had gone rampant far too long. In trying to force a plea from him, the sheriff slowly crushed him, having six men place heavy stones on his chest, yet still he refused to acknowledge the charge.

It's said that when the sheriff repeatedly demanded he plead guilty or innocent, Corey responded by asking for more weight, which the sheriff gladly provided. After two days, he died for his silence.

If Sunny fed the cops her *Desert Assassin* story, how well would I do in a tiny community like Burnham, where everyone is already distrustful of outsiders? Where nothing changes for years and years and one day a boy is murdered less than a week after I've arrived in town?

Would they believe me, a loner kid from the big city, or would they believe Sunny, the girl from just over in La Mesa who would surely put on her sweetest *I just knew he was trouble* face?

* * *

The road leading into the Dropouts was obviously not the route for me to take, as there was no place to hide from the moonlight or the high-beams of the occasional passing vehicle, and I would be spotted easily. I decided to sneak in from the north, on a trail that hugged the hillside and provided a little cover.

The ground under my sneakers crunched as I walked, and I wished I'd been wearing something warmer. The ninety-something-degree days usually gave way to pretty chilly nights, and I hadn't been home to grab anything extra to wear since that afternoon. The cold sweat that broke out whenever I thought of what Sunny could have done to Dayle didn't help the situation any.

The lights of the Dropouts came into view and I stopped to plan my route. There were a few spots where I'd have to cross from place to place out in the open, but I thought maybe I could get to the part of the village where Sunny kept her tent without being too exposed. Of course, Mr. Heath would be watching—though he'd be on the lookout for Sunny, not for me.

I scurried through the shadows along the perimeter, keeping mostly behind RVs and some of the bigger tents. When I came to the northern edge by the woodpile and solar panels, my legs became weak and wobbly, and my stomach wanted to empty itself again, right at the same spot where it had the last time I'd been there. I saw the place where Sunny had buried it, and I had to admit she did a good job of covering it up. You'd never know my breakfast from last week was just a foot below the surface.

It was hard not to speculate if Sunny could bury whole *people* that well. I suspected she could, if she wanted to, and the thought pushed me onward to the western border of the Dropouts, close to Sunny's tent.

I crept up behind a car, a station wagon with wood grain panels along the side, parked next to a trailer. I guess it had been *left* there more than *parked*, since a *parked* car sort of implies that it will be driven away again. This thing wasn't going anywhere, ever. All four tires were flat, the windshield was a spider web of cracks, and the sun had bleached most of the dashboard, originally maroon vinyl, to a pale pink.

Mr. Heath's car was parked far beyond Sunny's tent in a part of the village she likely wouldn't see if she came in from the south like he apparently expected her to. But I knew that if she were to come back here she'd do the same as me: walk the perimeter and scope it all out before making a move, and she would see his car just as I had. I shuddered at the thought that Sunny and I might do even the most trivial things the same way.

His car was easy enough to spot, but I couldn't find Mr. Heath anywhere. His silhouette didn't appear behind the wheel of his car, nor did he seem to be anywhere out in the open, though I didn't expect him to be. He'd have hidden himself—but were?

There were plenty of tents nearby he could have taken cover in, but it had gotten late enough that none of them would be empty—everyone would be inside for the night, and if he was inside one of them, he'd no doubt be talking to the occupants, and it was quiet enough to hear the occasional passing car all the way up on the main road. He wasn't in any of these tents.

Well, there was *one* tent I knew was empty.

And it was suddenly obvious, embarrassingly so, that Mr. Heath was waiting for his daughter right there inside her own tent. Probably sitting on the very mattress under which her cash was still hidden, waiting for her to come claim it.

Shit.

While I was no military strategist, I had read enough about war to recognize that what I needed was a *diversion*. And so I crept back along the way I had come until I was out of sight of Sunny's tent and within a dozen yards of Mr. Heath's car.

The driver's side faced away from where I expected Mr. Heath would be, and while it was hard to see much through the fabric of the tent I had to assume that a little light could get through. So if I wanted to open this car door, I knew the interior light would come on as soon as I opened it even a little, so I'd have to get to the dome light and shut that sucker off as quickly as possible.

Crouching next to the door, I peered through the window and saw the light—small, white frosted plastic, mounted on the roof between the front seats. I saw the little black switch on the forward edge of it, and in one smooth motion I opened the car door and reached inside, snapping the light off. It couldn't have been lit for more than half a second, but I waited, frozen, for the flap of Sunny's tent to tear open and Mr. Heath to come barreling out.

A full minute passed before I felt it was safe to move on to step two.

Still crouching, I reached over the driver's seat and found the parking brake handle, and pushed the chrome button on the end all the way in with my thumb. I lowered the handle, releasing the parking brake—the car rolled backwards by a couple of inches before settling, but it did so soundlessly.

On to step three, James.

The car was, lucky for me, a stick shift, and I simply yanked the shifter backwards until it popped out of gear and into neutral.

Mr. Heath's Chevy eased backwards an inch, then another, then another. As it rolled it picked up momentum and I straightened the steering wheel, putting it on a path toward one of the boulders at the end of the road before I ran off for cover in the shadows of the village's western edge. I circled behind the tents near Sunny's, staying low, moving quietly.

I heard the car hit the boulder about ten seconds later (the signature *crunch* of crumpling sheet metal and plastic taillights) and about two seconds after *that* Mr. Heath came rocketing out of Sunny's tent, his gaze following the tracks in the dust leading from where his car had *been* to where it now *was*, the rear bumper and trunk formed like scrunched paper around a twenty-ton chunk of sandstone at the end of the dirt road. His hands rose slowly, clutching either side of his head as though it would roll of his shoulders if he didn't hold it down.

As Mr. Heath trudged to his car I slipped behind him into the tent, barely registering anything around me except for the mattress, which I lifted with one hand while snatching the cash with the other. I jammed it into my front pocket and darted back outside, sprinting into the darkness behind the tents and RV's.

As I ran Mr. Heath called out his daughter's name, probably having heard me as I tore through the tent flaps and sprinted over the gravel, headed north.

He didn't bother to follow me.

* * *

I slowed down after I'd run maybe a quarter-mile, my legs burning, my lungs ready to burst. It felt like a spear had pierced my side, its point jammed under my ribs.

As I came to a stop—bent over with my hands on my thighs, knees locked, wheezing—it occurred to me that I still didn't know where I was going. I had the money, and somewhere out there Sunny had Dayle. The trade would go a lot smoother if I knew where the hell I was supposed to be.

A safe place in the middle of a very dangerous spot.

I stood tall and scanned the area around me, all three hundred and sixty degrees. This was *all* a dangerous spot. That's what the desert *is* at night.

But it finally came to me, and I realized there was one place in particular out here that was more perilous than the rest, and if one could manage to get to it, there was a perfectly safe point right in the middle.

I touched the spot where the cash bulged in my front pocket, reassured it was still there, and took off to rescue Dayle.

KF: When Sunny threatened you, when she said that Dale and Luke Pelletier would have more in common than living in a boring shithole town, what do you think she meant by that?

JM: She was saying that Dale would be dead. That's what they'd have in common. Both dead.

KF: Oh, right.

MD: I should've figured that one out on my own.

JM: I agree.

KF: James, I want to, um, I want to just throw this out there, just to satisfy my own curiosity. And we've said before, you know, we're not pointing any fingers at anyone, and I mean we're still just trying to get the whole story sorted out. But let's just say, for argument's sake, let's say your friend Sunny had it right. Like, what if you really did have it in for the Pelletier boy, and what if maybe you're a better marksman with that slingshot than you say. I don't mean to—

JM: Whoa.

DM: Should we maybe be getting a lawyer right now?

JM: I don't need a lawyer, I didn't do anything wrong dad.

DM: Being innocent doesn't mean you don't need—

KF: Look, you're obviously entitled

to have legal representation here, but I mean, that will kind of turn this into a whole big thing, and right now it's just us guys sitting around having a talk. We're not accusing James of anything or—

DM: Sounds to me like you are.

KF: No, Mr. Madison, we're not putting any blame for that boy's death on your son, and we're certainly not charging him, or anyone else as yet, with anything at all.

MP: We're just talking.

KF: We're just sitting here having a conversation to clear up some confusion and close any gaps in, you know, in our timeline of things.

JM: It's fine dad.

KF: It's just that, you know, I have bosses, we all do, and they're going to want to make sure that I looked at every angle, turned over every stone. And no, I mean I don't think your son acted malicious in any way when it comes to the death of Luke Pelletier, or that he was responsible for any of the... of the bloodshed that came after, but I report to people who will want to know that I went down that road and asked those questions.

DM: Okay. That's fine, whatever.

JM: Yeah.

KF: Okay, great then. Before we continue, does anybody need a bathroom break, or coffee or anything? Water?

DM: I wouldn't mind a quick break.

KF: Sure, the men's room is out that way and down... yeah, there you go.

JM: I'll go too.

KF: Okay meet back here in five?

MP: I think it's going good, Keith.

KF: Yeah. The kid's hard to read but I think we're making some headway. As long as he doesn't lawyer up too soon I think we have

(The recorder is turned off for an indeterminate time)
###

Chapter 27

The moon had risen high overhead by the time I reached the Buick. Where everything under the bright daytime sky was either olive or smoky tan, the midnight moon turned the landscape a silvery blue, cool and clean. A chilly breeze stirred up the dust around my feet, carrying it off somewhere to the southeast.

Even from a distance I could see my guess was correct, that Dayle was perched precariously in the only safe place in the area. She sat, her arms wrapped tightly around her knees, right on the roof of the Buick.

I came about a dozen yards from the old car before I heard the first rattle—it made me jump and I gasped, frozen in place. It wasn't much of a rattle, a small snake to be sure, but isn't there something they always say about the small snakes being the most venomous?

Probably not. But still, I waited for a moment to let my heart settle down to a survivable pace, breathing in, breathing out. *Get yourself under control,* I thought. *Relax, James.*

"Relax, James." Sunny's voice pierced the darkness as she stepped from the shadows of a low Joshua tree, and I jumped. "Just chill. Everyone will be just fine if you just chill."

My heart was back to beating double-time. "I wish you'd stop doing that," I said.

"Doing what?" She cocked her head to one side and pouted, shrugged her shoulders. "I don't know what you mean."

"You know what I mean," I said. "You scare the hell out of me every time you do that."

She laughed, stomping her foot and stirring up the rattlesnakes. The harder she stomped, the louder the rattles. On the roof of the Buick, Dayle whimpered. "You startle so easily," Sunny said. "I can't help it."

I rolled my eyes and hoped she saw.

"Now hand over my cash so I can get that whiney bitch out of my life," Sunny said. "I'm almost hoping you didn't bring it, just so I can kill her." She paused. "I think she might be afraid of snakes, James."

"No, no, here. Look—" I shoved my hand deep into my front pocket and pulled out a fistful of bills. "Look, it's all there. Whatever was under your mattress, it's all there. I didn't count it or anything, but—"

"I trust you," she said. "I mean, I trust that you know I'll murder you if there's even a nickel missing. There isn't a nickel missing, is there, James?"

"N-no. No, it's all there, every penny is there."

"Hand it over, then."

I shook my head. "Dayle first. Let Dayle go, then I'll give you the money." I crossed my arms and tried to lift my chin, pull my shoulders back and stand up tall but I was pretty sure she knew I was terrified of her.

"Look at you, James. Chivalry is alive and well, I guess. Fine, then—go get your stupid girlfriend." She nodded toward the Buick then stared off toward the Dropouts, where every camp was dark. I looked over at where Dayle sat and swallowed hard.

"How am I supposed to... I mean, the snakes."

"Jesus, James. Grow a set of balls and walk up to the damned thing, climb up onto the hood and rescue your girlfriend like a real man. I *put* her there, kicking and screaming, and I made it through just fine. I think you can handle it."

I'd never been any closer to the Buick than I already was right then. "Yeah, okay," I said. I doubt the tremor in my voice escaped Sunny's notice.

"You'll probably have to carry her—she'll never climb down off there on her own. That chick's a mess, James."

Dayle never was one to take an unnecessary risk, that was true.

I watched as my feet took their first steps towards the car, moving purposefully over the silver-blue sand, moving first to the left then right to avoid walking into a mound of brush. I glanced upward quickly to gauge my progress and was relieved to see I still had a ways to go.

Left, right. Left, right.

I lifted my head and stole a glance at the Buick: halfway there. Head down, right then left, around another mound of brush.

Suddenly I was close enough to hear Dayle breathing. It was a soft sound, an inhale-exhale touched by the quiver of her chest as she tried not to cry. I looked up and saw she was pursing her lips.

Right, Left.

Then from over my shoulder, a small stone rocketed through the moonlight and struck the trunk of the car with a *crack*. Sunny laughed as it ricocheted into the shadows, the snakes making their presence known. All of them together sounded like a rain stick—one of those long pieces of hollow wood with dried beans inside, when you stand it on its end and the beans cascade down through little passages inside the bamboo, trickling down, and it's supposed to sound like rain. But really, I just think it sounds like rattlesnakes.

Dayle cried out, startled, then covered her mouth with both hands, stifling a scream. Her eyes darted to the side and her gaze met mine. I knew it wouldn't do any good to tell her she was perfectly safe up there; she was near hysterical and reason wasn't in her playbook just yet.

Ten more steps and I reached the Buick. The snakes were quiet again—or at least they would be until I climbed on top of their home. I paused to consider my next move and tried to look confident while doing so, but the best I could manage was shaking like a Chihuahua with my hands on my hips.

Before I could really think about what I was doing I put one foot on the hood and then the other until I was standing upright somewhere over the carburetor. I could see straight down through the gap where the windshield once was, down into the pit of the old Buick's interior where the rattlers hid from the sun during the day. At night most of them were elsewhere, looking for something small and furry to eat.

Most, but not *all*.

"Give me your hand," I said to Dayle. "Stand up, give me your hand."

Dayle stayed right where she was.

"Come on," I said. "Just give me your hand and take one step down to me, and I'll carry you the rest of the way."

She lifted her gaze to meet mine, the offer of a safe lift out of the situation apparently worth considering, and rose on wobbling legs. I put one arm around her waist, the other behind her knees, and lifted her up like I was carrying a baby.

A big, heavy baby who kept slipping down through my arms.

"We'll be out of here in a minute," I told her,

and braced myself for stepping down off the hood and onto the dirt. "Hold onto me so you don't slide down."

She clung tightly to me, her arms wrapped around my neck, her face buried in my shoulder. In any other circumstance, I'd be pretty content with the whole arrangement.

I crouched as low as I could and let my feet slip down the front edge of the hood and onto solid ground, but as short as the drop was, the landing was still jarring and Dayle dug her fingers into the back of my neck to keep from falling. I gritted my teeth and took the longest strides possible away from the sudden burst of rattles that resonated from inside the car.

Ahead, Sunny clapped slowly in mock congratulations. "Good job, James. You're a big hero."

Before I'd even put Dayle back on her feet, Sunny held out her left hand. "Money now," she said.

I lowered Dayle carefully to the ground, letting her get her feet under her and holding her steady until she seemed okay on her own. Then I reached into my front pocket.

"We have a deal," I said.

"Yes James, we have a deal."

"I give you the money and you leave us alone for good."

"Sure, whatever. Money now."

I hesitated. Obviously, Sunny wasn't quite *trustworthy*, but something in her voice didn't leave me confident that she'd keep her word.

"James," she said. "This right here is Plan A. In Plan A, I snatch your bitch girlfriend, hold on to her until you get my cash for me, then I disappear to who knows where and you two can do whatever you want because who gives a shit—I'll be gone. Talk to the cops 'til you're blue in the face, it won't matter to me once I'm clear of this dustbowl."

"If this is Plan A—"

"You would *not* like Plan B," she said.

I was afraid to ask, but I asked anyway. "What happens in Plan B?"

"That would be a murder-suicide, James. The way I figure it, little Dayle found out what you did to that poor boy behind the woodpile, added it all up and realized what a *murderer* you were, so you had no choice but to keep her quiet by suffocating her with a plastic bag over her head. Like this one." Sunny produced a white plastic bag from her back pocket, the kind they bag your groceries in at the general store. The fact that she'd actually *brought* one with her in case she needed to go to *Plan B* made me break out in a cold sweat.

"Then, of course, overcome with grief and guilt, you cut your own wrist," she continued, "and bled out, sitting under that tree right there, that Joshua tree, which I always thought would look nice —you all bloodless and slumped against that tree. It new life somewhere else, leaving what little she owns behind, with no place to live and no easy way to get there.

In Plan B, she stages a murder-suicide, and the only witnesses to what really happened to Luke Pelletier are silenced forever. The only obstacle to what Sunny called *back to normal* would be her father, who she could simply elude for a few more days until he gave up and moved on, or she could kill him too, and probably have little trouble getting away with it.

I felt the bills crinkle as my fist closed around them in my pocket.

With Plan B, she wouldn't have to leave here, she wouldn't have to start over. No one even suspects her of *anything* at this point, and she'd still be under the radar while the whole mess got sorted out. She'd have her money, her home, her peace and quiet.

I pulled the money from my pocket and watched myself extend my hand, holding the cash out for Sunny to take.

Why in the world would she choose Plan A? Even *I* would have gone for the murder-suicide scheme, and I'm not even a sociopath.

Still, in slow motion, I uncurled my fingers and Sunny reached for the cash. But instead of taking the money from my open hand, she suddenly grabbed me by the wrist, her other hand appearing from behind her, where it had been casually tucked would look good from over that way, where the cops would first see you. It's framed nice, you know, with the Buick in the background, the hills over that way filling in the negative space and all."

She smiled, almost dreamily. "It would make a pretty good postcard," she added.

I searched for something to say and came up empty. She had it so...*planned out.*

"After that, all I'd have to do is deal with my father and everything would be back to normal."

"Normal?" I asked.

"Like it was before you came to town, James. Before you showed up I had it made, I had peace and quiet and nobody looking for me. Okay, maybe I was a little bored but all in all it was pretty much a paradise." She stared me down, blinked once. "Money now."

I've heard that in times of stress or in an emergency, your thought process can speed up. Like when people in car crashes later say it seemed to happen in slow motion, that's because they were processing it faster than normal so everything around them appeared to slow down.

As I reached into my pocket for the money, I began to compare Plans A and B.

In Plan A, I give her the money that was in her tent, the money she couldn't easily get to because her dad was watching, waiting for her to show up and claim it. When she has the money, she leaves Dayle and me alone and disappears to start a into her back pocket. I saw, too late to react, that she gripped a pocketknife, the blade catching my eye like the flash of a camera as the moon momentarily reflected its glow in the polished steel.

Her hand still seized my wrist like a welder's vise, the pressure probably causing pain but I wasn't feeling *anything* at that moment. Her right hand shot towards me, and she deftly drew the blade across my left forearm, the shiny edge sinking deep into my skin, down into muscle.

That, I felt.

Chapter 28

At first it was a distant sting, a surface wound. But as the blood began to run down to my wrist and drip from my fingers it became more of an *ache*, the deep throbbing of my vein emptying.

Sunny released my wrist and placed her hand flat on my chest, pausing for a moment to wink before giving me a hard push backwards. I stumbled once and fell against the serrated trunk of the Joshua tree, landing hard in the dirt. I cradled my wounded arm, staring dumbly as the warm blood pooled in my cupped hand.

It didn't make sense. This wasn't the kind of thing that's supposed to happen to me.

I wondered how many handfuls of blood were in me, and how many would have to run out through my wrist before I started to feel faint. How many handfuls would I lose before I couldn't think clearly? How many before my heart didn't have enough blood in it to bother beating and just stopped like a broken watch?

Dayle stared at me, unbelieving. She swayed slightly, and even in the dark I could tell that she'd gone pale.

I knew how she felt.

Julius Caesar had been stabbed twenty-three times. According to the autopsy—the earliest ever recorded—it was the second wound that had proved fatal.

Sunny loomed above me, her features darkened against the moonlit sky. She rubbed the handle of the knife against her shirt, careful to wipe each surface, then holding it by the lightest of fingertips, dropped it in my lap.

Instinctively, I picked it up. It felt too small to have made that wound in my forearm. It felt cheap, lightweight and I somehow managed, despite everything that was happening, to be offended that I may have just been murdered with such a ridiculous little pocket knife. I held it in my fist, blade up, as though I was waiting for a steak in a restaurant.

"Phase One, complete," Sunny said, then pulled the plastic bag from her back pocket and shook it open loudly. "On to Phase two."

She turned to Dayle, still staring at me, frozen in shock, and spun her by the shoulders until she had her back turned to us before pulling the plastic bag down over Dayle's head and twisting it closed tightly in her fist. She stood like a boxer, feet wide for stability, her back straight as Dayle suddenly snapped out of her daze and fought for her life, clawing at the bag where it tightened around her neck.

If she'd relaxed a bit and thought it through, Dayle would've ripped a hole in the bag near her mouth so she could breathe instead of trying to pull the whole thing off. But you don't think straight when you're panicked and suffocating, I guess.

It went on forever, Dayle struggling while Sunny just stood there, solidly, hanging on to the twisted-up ends of the bag and waiting. The bag inflated, then collapsed over her face as Dayle breathed in, breathed out, over and over.

Inflate, collapse. Inflate, collapse.

This wasn't supposed to happen to Dayle, either. Things like this don't happen to nice girls from Burnham. Girls from Burnham graduate high school and go to college in San Diego, then move to New York City for a few years before the winters beat them down and they come back to the west coast and have a family.

Dying in the desert is for jackrabbits and Las Vegas gangsters.

Finally, Dayle slowed. Her fight slowed, her breathing slowed, and as she sunk to the ground, Sunny still keeping a tight hold on the bag over her head, Dayle came to a full stop altogether.

I was starting to feel the blood loss. My skin felt cold and the stars spun above me. The knife slid out of my hand and into the dirt.

Sunny crouched next to Dayle, studying her face. Then she turned her head and studied my face too. Her expression showed no emotion other than curiosity.

"Between you and me," Sunny said, "the very first moment I saw Dayle, I knew I was going to strangle the bitch."

I just stared. That's about all I had the energy for.

"You know how sometimes you meet somebody, and you just *know* you're going to murder them? You know that feeling? I have it all the time." She smiled. "You, though—I really didn't see this coming. I thought we were friends, James." Her smile vanished and her eyes narrowed. "I thought we were going to be good together."

I lowered my eyes and watched the bag over Dayle's face. It was still. Far away, a coyote howled, and ever farther away, another one answered.

How long would it take after I was dead before the coyotes came around? How long until they fought over me, snapping and snarling at each other while they pulled me apart and dragged little pieces of me off to their cubs or curled up in their den with a piece of bone to gnaw on?

I had never thought of myself as meat before.

Would I still be a person when I was in little pieces? A chicken is still chicken when it's cut up into wings and thighs in the grocery store.

But then, there is a difference between *chicken* and *a* chicken. One runs around clucking and pecking at the ground and the other is great when roasted in the oven with garlic and rosemary and a splash of white wine.

I could almost smell the garlic.

If a cow becomes beef, and a pig becomes pork, what does a person become?

What would I be called when I stopped being James Lewis Madison and became food?

I knew this. It's...I read a book about French Polynesia the year before and it had a chapter on cannibalism and they called it...*long pig*.

Cow is to beef as human is to long pig.

Sunny snapped her fingers in front of my face. How long had I let my mind wander? She was smiling again and looking at me like I was funny little fish in an aquarium. Like she might tap the glass at any moment.

Blood overflowed my cupped hand and soaked into my jeans.

KF: One thing that bothers me, James. When Sunny was describing her plan B to you, the murder-suicide scenario, she said... let me see, she said... Dayle added it all up and realized what a murderer you were, so you had no choice but to keep her quiet. That's what I have in my notes.

JM: Okay.

KF: I don't get how, I mean, I don't understand what Dayle is adding up. What does she know, or think she knows I guess, that would lead her to the conclusion that the Pelletier boy's death wasn't an accident?

JM: I don't know.

KF: Well, it's an odd thing for Sunny to say, right?

JM: I guess, yeah.

KF: It just sort of stood out as something that didn't make sense.

JM: Sunny probably told Dayle the desert assassin thing, she probably got the murder motive thing from that.

KF: You think they chatted much, when Sunny was abducting Dayle?

JM: Well I don't think they actually—

KF: Yeah, I just don't really see it happening that way. It's kind of bothering me. But we can move on, if you want.

JM: Sure.

KF: Okay, then. Um... How about the knife, let's talk about the knife.

JM: What about it?

KF: We have it here—Mike, can you— yeah, that's the one. We have the knife here, James, this is the one, it was recovered from the scene, the area on the west side of route 48, south of Burnham.

JM: Okay.

KF: It was found next to the, next to one of the bodies. I'm sure it won't be any surprise to you that we were able to lift prints from it, and the only prints found anywhere on it are yours.

JM: Well, yeah. I mean I told you, Sunny wiped her prints off on her shirt after she cut my arm.

KF: Yes, you did mention that, but again, it's the little details that are bothering me here. Like... after she cut your arm, she dropped the knife in your lap. You picked it up, so your prints were then on it, which makes sense, sure, but then after...

MP: I think we're getting ahead, Keith. I think we should back up to the—no, wait, I have a question, if that's okay.

KF: Sure Mike.

MP: During your bathroom break I put a call in to the La Mesa PD, couldn't get my buddy from arson on the line yet but I did run something by them and found something interesting.

KF: Sure.

MP: This gorge in La Mesa, the one they pulled the dead girl from, the one who they assumed was Sunny?

JM: Kippels Gorge.

MP: Yeah, Kippels. Um, doesn't exist.

JM: What?

MP: No such thing. There isn't even a river that runs anywhere near La Mesa. No river, no gorge. Whoever came up with that whole story really didn't have the slightest idea of what La Mesa is like.

KF: Well, that's interesting.

MP: I'll say.

KF: you have any thoughts on that, James?

JM: I don't—I don't understand what that, what it means then.

KF: How so?

JM: If Mr. Heath made that part up, I don't know what that means for—I mean then he could have made everything up, for all we know. So I don't understand why, like, what the hell is going on now. I don't know why he would make something like that up.

MP: Maybe he didn't make it up.

JM: How do you mean?

MP: Maybe you made it up. Not him.

KF: Easy, Mike.

MP: I'm just conjecturing, is all.

KF: Yeah, I know. But let's dial it back a bit, okay? No need to get everyone all riled up, we're just talking it through, figuring out what happened.

MP: It's just that between that gorge story and the knife, Keith, there are some inconsistencies, is what I'm saying.

KF: Yeah, I know. It does raise up a few questions, doesn't it?

Chapter 29

Sunny grinned at me, apparently satisfied with her work, as Dayle lay in a heap on the ground a few feet away, the bag still pulled over her head. The bag had come open where Sunny had cinched it around Dayle's neck, but I supposed that didn't help Dayle much at this point.

"Any last requests?" Sunny asked me.

I stared at the wound in my arm, the blood still surfacing, and I could almost see the exact point where it flowed from the severed vein. "Cigarette," I croaked.

For the first time that night, Sunny was taken aback. "You didn't exactly enjoy your first one," she said. "Almost barfing and all."

"Cigarette," I repeated.

Sunny shrugged and reached into her back pocket, producing a crushed pack of cigarettes, and slid one from the box. It was bent and creased, and she pushed the filtered end into the corner of her mouth, the cigarette bouncing up and down as she spoke.

"I guess it's kind of classic, isn't it? The last smoke. Although—" She lit the cigarette for me with a few flicks of her blue lighter, took a drag, then tucked it between my lips. "I doubt you'll live long enough to see the last drag. You're bleeding out pretty fast."

She looked at me with what I expected to be pity but instead was simple curiosity, staring deep into my eyes and looking for fear of death, or defeat —who knows what she wanted to see.

"Adios, James," she said. "Happy trails." Sunny turned on her heels and bounded, almost skipping, to the east.

* * *

I puffed on the cigarette, trying hard not to breathe it in. Still, I coughed.

The more I puffed, the brighter the end glowed, getting hotter and hotter. Hot enough so I could feel the warmth hit my nose.

I squinted as the smoke rolled up my face, trying to keep it from getting in my eyes, and studied the slice in my arm. It was a clean cut—clean and deep. I pulled the wound open as far as I could with my right hand until I saw the vein itself, until I was lightheaded, seeing stars as the pain tore through my forearm, radiating to my hand, up to my shoulder. I tilted my head back and took a deep breath until the stars faded and the sky stopped spinning.

I took a few more drags on the cigarette. Everything around me sparkled and spun, and I couldn't tell if it was because of the nicotine or the blood loss.

Spreading the wound open with my finger and thumb, I lowered my head until the blaze-orange end of the cigarette touched the open end of the severed vein. There was a quiet hiss as the cigarette threatened to go out, turning a dark amber color, but through the electrifying burst of searing pain I puffed away on the cigarette until it glowed again.

I leaned back against the Joshua tree, catching my breath, still squinting from the smoke. More stars, more spinning. My left arm felt like it had been sawed off just below the elbow, the raw stump splashed with gunpowder.

Strangely, I didn't scream. I didn't even cry, I just ground my teeth, chewing on the filter, my head buried in the knotty, clenched muscles of my good arm, my right hand balled into a tight fist. I groaned through pursed lips.

When I thought I could lower my head and remain conscious, I inspected my wound. The blood running down my arm had slowed, but it still trickled out, and I wasn't sure if it was because I had managed to seal up the vein somewhat or if I was just running out of blood to lose.

A few more drags, and I went back in.

This hiss, the burn, the stars and the spinning. This time I *did* scream, but it was partly in triumph, because I was sure I'd sealed off the vein. *Cauterized* it, as the doctors would say.

The ancient Romans *cauterized* wounds with red-hot irons or boiling oil.

I took a few more deep breaths to get my senses back, and pulled my tee shirt over my head, wrapping it tightly over the gash in my arm and knotting it as best as I could to keep it from unraveling. I crawled to Dayle on my hands and knees.

She had no pulse. Or if she did, I couldn't find it. I pulled the bag from her head, studying her face, and couldn't tell if her skin had turned blue or if she just *looked* blue in the moonlight. I rolled her onto her back, straightened out her legs and started CPR.

They'd taught us how to perform CPR in our health class at school during my freshman year. They'd taught us *a lot* of things I never expected to use, like how to calculate the volume of a cylinder or what a possessive pronoun is. But CPR seemed like a skill that would actually be worth having, so I paid attention.

Interesting fact: the ideal rate for chest compressions while performing cardiopulmonary resuscitation is around one hundred pumps per minute. The easiest way to get and stay on this pace is to play a song in your head with a similar tempo, and the easiest song to remember for such an occasion is probably the BeeGees' *Stayin' Alive*.

Another song with a tempo perfect for CPR

is Queen's *Another One Bites the Dust.*

Thirty pumps to Dayle's chest, then two breaths, then thirty pumps, then two breaths. Over and over, no quitting, no giving up.

I worried that my amateur cigarette surgery wouldn't hold up through the compressions, that any one pump would be one too many and blood would start rushing down my wrist again and there I'd be without a lit cigarette to cauterize the wound.

So I was careful. But I didn't need to worry, because after a minute or so my blood had stayed inside where it belonged and Dayle coughed a little and opened her eyes.

There was no miraculous gasp when she awoke, no sputtering to life, clinging to me in gratitude. She opened her eyes very slowly, just barely enough to let the light in at first, then a little wider, pupils pointed straight ahead, aimed somewhere in the sky above us.

I said her name. She didn't respond, just stared upwards into the stars. I worried there might have been brain damage, with her having gone for so long without oxygen.

Then she spoke, softly, and to herself: "Am I dead?"

"Not anymore," I said.

Chapter 30

She couldn't walk more than a few steps without stumbling, so I carried her, like I had when I'd taken her down from the roof of the Buick. Or when we'd been caught in that dust storm a few years back.

Her arms didn't wrap around my neck like they had before, they just rested in her lap as we went. Her head rolled from side to side with each step though the desert as I carried her towards the main road.

Dayle had to be okay. There had to be a limit to the damage Sunny could do, it had to stop somewhere. I'd managed to survive, and Dayle was breathing again. I had to make sure that it never got any worse than it already had.

I'd already allowed things to go too far. I didn't know when it was, but there had to have been a point when I could have taken some kind of action, made some kind of decision, that would have headed all of this off and prevented this night from going so wrong.

I supposed that when Sunny wanted me to scare Luke with the slingshot I could have said *no*. That would have been the way to go.

In retrospect.

Live and learn.

As small as Dayle was, carrying her over the sand for a half-mile to the nearest point on Route 48 was a major feat of strength. My back ached, my legs shook. As we approached the road, my wound reopened, the blood seeping into Dayle's shirt.

With each step she slipped lower and lower in my arms, but I wouldn't drop her. She was too weak to hold on to me, too dazed from being oxygen-deprived to understand what was happening, and I really wasn't in much better shape. But *I* was the only one who had any control over the situation, *I* was the only one who could keep the night from getting any worse, and *I* was not going to screw it up.

When we finally reached the asphalt I set her down as gently as I could, relieved to see her sitting upright, looking around, aware of her surroundings.

"Break time," I said, and sat next to her to rewrap my tee shirt over my wounded wrist. "I'll flag down the next car that comes along and get us a ride to the hospital."

She nodded, all of her drawn inward, shaking. "I want to stand up," she said. "I'm gonna puke."

"Oh—sure, sure." I helped her up with my right hand, the left too slick with blood to be of any use. Her legs wobbled under her, but she stood on her own. Like a newborn faun.

She didn't puke, she just stood there shaking

and staring vacantly into the night.

There was no question that my wound had reopened, and all I had with me to stop the blood was my already-blood-soaked tee shirt. I wrapped it tighter around my forearm, hoping that would be enough to slow the bleeding and keep me conscious until a car came along.

"I'm sorry," I said.

"What?"

"I'm sorry," I repeated. "For everything that's happened tonight."

Dayle kept staring into the darkness. Maybe she nodded.

The night air was chilly, the right weather for a coat or a hoodie but I was naked from the waist up. It probably didn't help that I'd lost most of my blood, too, and I shook, unable to control the spasms that ran through me.

Dayle stood next to me, and she shook too. She was dressed warmer than I was, and I figured she probably had the shakes from recently being murdered and brought back to life. Hard to figure what someone's reaction to something like that might be.

A tremor seemed reasonable.

It seemed like forever since the last time I'd been in my room back home, in our apartment in Boston. It felt like a year had gone by. But it had only been, what—six days? Seven?

I missed my room in our apartment. I

missed my mom. I missed daylight for some reason, and if granted one wish I probably would have wanted it to be a bright, sunny city morning instead of this endless, black desert night. Things are always better in the daylight.

My throat tightened and suddenly I knew I was about to cry. I turned away from Dayle so she wouldn't see.

"Car," Dayle said, looking to the north.

I heard it before I saw it: the hum of an engine, the hiss of tires over a dusty road. Suddenly headlights broke from behind a rocky berm, the black silhouette of a sedan trailing behind.

I wiped a few tears from my face and shielded my eyes from the glare, trying to see past the lights and into the driver's seat. By the time I could see who was at the wheel, the car was already upon us. It rolled to a stop and I got to my feet, standing close to Dayle. I put my good arm around her shoulders and pulled her to me.

Mr. Heath called to me from the idling car. "James Madison, I'm surprised to see you. Need a lift?"

Chapter 31

The rear-end of his car was crumpled, the brake lights smashed, the trunk lid sort of half-opened. Still, the Chevy was drivable, despite the sound of some bent panel or trim rubbing against one of the tires.

He reached across the empty front seat and opened the passenger-side door. I walked Dayle the few steps toward it and sat her down, then I slid into the darkened back seat behind her.

"I suppose I don't need to introduce you to my daughter, Rebecca," he said.

There she was, sitting in the back, inches from me. All I saw was her silhouette in the dark of the sedan's interior, but I knew she was smiling by the way the backlit outline of her cheeks rose a little.

"Damn, James," she whispered. "You're a friggin' *trooper.*"

In the rearview mirror I saw Mr. Heath studying me, his brow creased. "You both look like you need medical attention," he said. "What happened?"

I stole a glance at Sunny and she shrugged. "What *did* happen, James?"

"Long story," I said.

Mr. Heath ran his thumb over his mustache,

studying Dayle, thoughtful. "Well, whatever happened, you two need to see a doctor. Closest place to get you checked out at this hour is the emergency clinic in Mejias, and I don't mind bringing you. In fact, I insist on it. Twenty minutes south. Hope you're okay with a bit of a ride."

I sunk down into the seat and did my best to pretend there could be a happy ending to the night.

"I was just on my way out of town when I saw Rebecca crossing the road a ways back," he said. "So I scooped her up, and now I find you two looking like the living dead in the middle of nowhere."

In the mirror, his gaze turned from me to his daughter. "I'm hoping it's just coincidence," he said.

Sunny remained silent.

"Because if it's not, that's more than I can take, Becca. I'm willing to overlook a few things, you know, because of what your mother did to you all those years. But you have no excuses out here. You got yourself a clean start and there's no reason for blood now."

Sunny turned to face the window, glaring at the desert.

"When these two get to the clinic and doctors start asking them how they ended up all bloody and half-catatonic, what will they say, Becca?"

"You can't take them to any clinic," she replied.

"I have to," Mr. Heath said. "I picked them up, it's my responsibility."

Sunny let out a long sigh. "Fine. But pull over for a sec, I think James is gonna barf."

The car was already slowing and drifting towards the side of the road when he looked into the mirror at me. "You doing okay back there, James?"

I looked from Mr. Heath to Sunny and back. "What?"

Sunny put a finger to her lips and winked. "*Shh.*"

Before the car had even come to a full stop, Sunny leaned forward in her seat, the little pocketknife in her hand, and raked it smoothly across her father's neck, from his left ear to the hollow under his chin all the way his right ear.

"I told you," she said softly. "You can't take them to any clinic."

Chapter 32

Mr. Heath grabbed his neck with both hands. Blood ran over his fingers and wrists, making black rivers in the shadows of the car's interior. He gasped and wheezed, and in the mirror I saw his eyes like shiny white coins gaping at me.

The sedan came to a lethargic stop, the engine still running, the headlights casting their beams far into the desert flats. I smelled Mr. Heath's blood as he slumped sideways, gracelessly, toward the passenger side.

"Out of the car," Sunny said to me.

Before I could even move, the passenger door flew open and Dayle climbed out, still wobbly but able to keep her legs under her. She teetered off into the night, running for her life into the darkness.

Sunny kicked her door open, muttering *Jesus Christ* before jogging around the front of the car and taking off after Dayle.

I watched through the window as Sunny ran into the same moonlit spot of the desert where Dayle had run, watched Sunny overtake her prey effortlessly, watched as she sunk the pocketknife's blade as far as it would go into the back of Dayle's neck.

Stars appeared at the edges of my vision, and

the car seemed to levitate and spin. I felt nauseated and opened the door, leaning out just in time to empty my stomach into the dirt.

I lifted my head in time to see Dayle fall facedown behind a mound of scrub, Sunny standing over her in victory. She kicked Dayle once in the leg, and getting no response, walked back to the car.

Even with my head hanging out the door in the fresh air I could still smell Mr. Heath's blood. It hit my nose like warm, wet copper. My own blood was still seeping through the shirt I'd wrapped around my arm, more sticky now than slick.

Sunny's sneakers appeared in the dirt outside the car door and I looked up. She towered over me, a look of annoyance on her face.

"Let's try this again," she said, and cleared her throat. "Sunny murders James, take two—although it doesn't look like I have to do much more than just let you finish dying on your own."

She grabbed a fistful of my hair and pulled until I clambered off of the seat and out into the night air. I fell hard onto my knees in the gravel, the pain distant and filtered. Everything, in fact, had slowly become distant and filtered, and it felt almost as though I wasn't in control of my own body—it felt more like I was just an observer.

She stood me up, walked me out to where Dayle lay. I knew this time, I could feel it, that Dayle was dead. A narrow trail of crimson ran from a tiny wound in the back of her neck, and her eyes were open, though sightless and already bearing a thin film of Burnham dust.

"Jesus," I heard myself say.

Sunny stood over me, hands on her hips. She looked so tall from where I lay, like her body stretched on forever, up into the stars.

By then my vision had become more sparkles than substance and the sky spun too fast for me to make sense of it and I fell. I landed on my side, my face toward the sky, my wounded arm splayed outward. The stars that had crowded my sight faded into darkness at the edges, with only a small circle of light at the center. Sunny's face appeared in the circle of light, looking at me from far above, her expression knowing and pitiless. She winked just before the darkness took over and I could see no more.

KF: You know, the nurse explained to us how you got those burns inside the wound on your arm, but I didn't really grasp it until you described it in detail like that. I'm a little queasy, James.

MP: Fucking gross, is what that was.

KF: Language, Mike.

MP: Right. But that's like, surgery from the dark ages.

JM: Misnomer.

MP: What?

JM: The dark ages aren't called that because they were dark or lacked civility. That period is called dark because of the lack of an historical record. It's less illuminated than, like, the Italian renaissance or the dynastic periods in Egypt. Which we know lots about.

KF: That's wonderful. Anyway, I think we have a lot to talk about here. A lot to talk about. Now, all that you just told us, just now, most of that is generally consistent with what our crime scene techs were able to piece together. Which is surprising to me, but we'll get to that in a bit. I still have some questions, and I think Mike does, too. Detective Perez I mean.

MP: I do.

KF: I want to revisit something we talked about earlier. The first time you went to the general store to see Dayle when you arrived in town for the summer. And you saw her with that boy.

JM: Right.

KF: And also, I want to ask you again, if you had ever seen Luke Pelletier before that day when you say Sunny teased him about his stutter.

JM: No, that was the first time I'd ever seen that kid.

MP: You're lying, James.

JM: No, I'm not.

KF: Easy, Mike. But the fact is, James, that the first time you saw Luke Pelletier was when he was sitting on the loading dock behind the general store with Dayle, and they were holding hands. That's what one of the store's employees told us. A woman, um, Shelby. You were right there, looking right at him, James. Right there.

MP: Miss Shelby told our detectives that Dayle was dating a boy named Luke Pelletier, and that he lived in the dropouts with his mother. She even described, him, and what she told us matched exactly the—

JM: But that—it wasn't the same kid, that was a different kid. That was Dayle's boyfriend.

KF: It was the very same boy, and you were no more than four or five feet away from him, according to what you told us.

JM: But I was down on the ground and they were sitting up above me on the dock, and I had to look up into the sun, so—I had a hard time—

KF: So you're saying the kid's face was obscured by the glare of the sun.

JM: Yes. That's what I'm saying.

MP: And then there's the slingshot. Where's the slingshot right now, James?

JM: I told you I don't know. Sunny took it I think. I don't know what she did with it.

KF: It would probably interest you to know that right after you told us about how you buried that cat, the cat you told us Sunny killed to make you look crazy and guilty, we radioed a couple of our guys who were already out that way to go to the area behind your father's property and check that out, to verify your story. I don't need to tell you what we found, Do I James?

JM: Actually you probably do.

KF: During your bathroom break it was brought to our attention that they found a slingshot down in that same hole along with the dead cat.

MP: Isn't that something.

KF: It sure is.

JM: Sunny must have put it there. There's no way. There's no way the slingshot is really there.

KF: It's not like we can run ballistics on a slingshot or anything, but it still doesn't make you look very good, James. Not very good at all. So you need to be straight with us, James, no more stories.

DM: I'm thinking this is a good time

for my son to ask for a lawyer.

MP: Is that what you want, James? A lawyer? Because the second you make that request this whole thing is no longer just a conversation. We'll book you, and take your clothes and take you away from your father and put you in a cell until God knows when.

KF: Easy, Mike.

JM: I don't need a lawyer because I didn't do anything wrong. Dad. I didn't.

DM: You can't threaten my son just because he wants representation.

KF: He just said he doesn't want representation, Mr. Madison. If he wants it, he'll ask for it. You can be present with him right now while we talk but as far as lawyers and such go that's his decision to make.

DM: Jesus Christ.

JM: Dad.

KF: Is anything you told us today the truth, James? Was there one true word in anything you've said? Because I look at my notes here, at what you've told me was the way everything happened, then I look at the evidence, and they don't mesh. They don't agree, James. They're inconsistent.

JM: Which are? What is—

KF: First of all, lying about knowing the victim of a murder is pretty telling. That's a textbook sign of guilt if there ever was one. And not only did you know who he was, the kid was in a relationship with the girl you admitted you'd always wanted to start a thing with.

JM: I never said that.

KF: But you did say that. And the murder weapon was just found very close to your father's property, in a hole that you yourself told us you dug.

JM: I told you, Sunny had to have dug the cat up and put it there. She had to.

MP: I'm getting tired of hearing about Sunny.

KF: We'll get to that, Mike. Also, James, there's the fact that you claim the kid's death was an accident, yet you failed to report it to the police.

JM: I told you why. I just sat here for like three hours, explaining why I didn't go to the cops.

MP: Because of Sunny.

JM: Yes.

KF: And then there's Neil, he owns the general store, he says he never had a problem with shoplifting until you arrived, James, and you know what items were stolen? I bet you do.

JM: I'm guessing it was a slingshot and ammo.

KF: Bingo. What else do we have, Mike?

MP: The knife.

KF: The knife, the pocketknife that cut your arm, the one Dayle was stabbed in the neck with. The one that very likely was used to slash Heath's throat. I don't need to tell you whose knife that was.

JM: Sunny's.

KF: That was Dayle's knife, James. Neil and Shelby both recognized that knife right off the bat as the one Dayle always had in her pocket at work for opening boxes when deliveries came. A little Swiss Army knockoff. This knife right here in the evidence bag.

MP: Man. Killed with her own knife.

KF: Did Sunny cut your arm, James, or does it maybe make more sense that Dayle was the one who cut your arm, cut it in self-defense? It was her knife, after all. Which makes more sense do you think?

JM: What?

DM: Seriously James, that lawyer. You should really ask for that lawyer.

KF: Makes the most sense to me that Dayle cut you. I think Dayle figured out you killed Luke Pelletier out of jealousy, and you murdered her before she could tell anyone. She fought back and put a good slice into your arm, even ran off a good distance before you took the knife away and sunk this blade here into her neck, right between her vertebra and into her spinal cord. Right here.

MP: Crime scene analysis seems to suggest that's exactly what happened you know.

KF: Footprints and blood don't lie, James. It's all spelled out in the sand, from that old car buried in the desert to where we found you all out by route 48. Footprints and blood.

MP: I think you made up a hell of a lot of what you told us today, James.

JM: You guys are fucking idiots. This is exactly what Sunny wanted you to think, that I was jealous and that I did it on purpose, she just wanted me to take the blame so she could run off with no one looking for her, she just—

MP: I bet if I gave you a slingshot and a handful of ammo you could hit a pop bottle from seventy yards. I bet you could put a dent in a quarter from that far. I bet you're a real sniper, like black ops and such.

JM: Seriously?

KF: Let's talk about Sunny, James. Now, when you were in the hospital we talked to most of the people in town. Interviewed as many people as we could. I'd say we talked to ninety percent of Burnham just yesterday.

MP: Everyone was real helpful, wanting to get to the bottom of the murders and everything.

KF: Guess how many of them remembered seeing you around town with anyone other than Dayle or your father?

JM: How many?

KF: Zero, James. Zero. All that time you spent with Sunny and not one person can say they saw you with her?

JM: We didn't really spend much time in town, we hung out mostly way out in the—

KF: That gorge in La Mesa doesn't exist, James. There isn't even a river there. There's no record of a house fire in the last year, or even farther back, that even remotely matches the events you say happened with Sunny's mother and father. That whole story, every last bit of it James, is fiction.

MP: My friend in arson was like, never happened.

JM: But Mr. Heath—

MP: Jesus Christ, James. Mr. Heath? Mr. Heath?

KF: Let's relax here, take a breath. This is the part that genuinely confuses me, and I think—I think the only answer here is that maybe you honestly, truly don't know, James, that you just don't understand. Everything else you could have just made up, real easy, but the Mr. Heath thing (inaudible) ...something you don't even know you created in your own mind. That's the only answer.

JM: What the hell are you talking about?

DM: Lawyer, James. For Christ's sake.

JM: I need to hear this first.

KF: James, the man we found at the wheel of the Chevy, the one with his throat cut. He wasn't Mr. Heath. He was Detective Heath.

JM: I don't understand.

MP: He was one of ours.

KF: The Chevy you described him

driving, James? That was his cruiser. It was unmarked, but it was still pretty clearly a State Police vehicle. Searchlight and everything. Big old radio. Hard to overlook something like that unless you're living in some made-up universe in your own head.

JM: This isn't making sense to me.

KF: He called in on the radio that he saw you on the side of the road, the night before last, he saw you with Dayle. She was running from you, he said. Running away, scared. He put her in the front seat and you in the back. Said you had lost a lot of blood and he was taking you both here to Mejias for medical and that he was going to book you for the murder of Luke Pelletier.

MP: You couldn't let him take you in, could you James? Had to kill him too, you little asshole.

KF: Mike.

MP: Heath said he had a real awkward interview with you in the dropouts, you were sneaking around there. Some of the dropouts people said they'd been missing money from their tents, thought you had something to do with it. He went there looking for more info on whatever else you might've been up to and happened to run right into you.

KF: He said you couldn't really explain what you were doing there. Said you claimed to be looking for a friend.

MP: A friend no one else around there had ever heard of.

JM: That's not right, that's not—he and I talked about Sunny, he told me about her. He...

KF: I know what Detective Heath reported about the events that night, James, and it's nothing like what you just told us.

MP: Nothing. That was the night you said he told you the story about Sunny faking her death and all. But right here in the record, it says he interviewed you about Luke Pelletier. You're delusional.

KF: James, the only thing that makes everything add up right, the only possible scenario, given the blood evidence, the fingerprints, eyewitnesses, is that you acted alone. That's the only thing that makes sense here.

JM: But that's not right, that's not what happened, how—Sunny planned this from—

KF: There is no Sunny, James. There never was. In a town like Burnham, with only, what, sixty houses in it, everyone knows everyone else. Intimately. And nobody ever mentioned a girl named Sunny, in all the interviews we did. Nobody said they'd ever seen anyone other than Dayle with you.

MP: Those times you say you met Sunny on the picnic table by the general store parking lot? Where's that notebook, Keith.

KF: Right here. Here.

MP: According to Shelby at the general store, several mornings you walked up from the main road and just sat by yourself on the picnic table, just staring off into nowhere. Said it gave her the creeps, you just sitting there alone. Then after a while you'd get up and walk off towards the dropouts.

KF: All by yourself.

MP: All by yourself. And the time you said you and Sunny stole money from one of the tents?

KF: You were seen by a woman named, here it is, Margaret Freeman and she says you were alone, James. She saw you coming out of Carlos Aguilar's tent, all by your lonesome.

JM: This isn't right.

KF: Three deaths, James. Luke Pelletier, Dayle Lynwood, Detective Marcus Heath. All on you.

MP: Not that the first two aren't serious enough, but killing a cop. Man.

KF: He just moved here, came down with his family from Seattle PD to work San Diego. He was a good man, a good cop. Didn't know him too well but he was a good cop.

JM: I'd like to speak with a lawyer now, please. I would like a lawyer.

(The recording concludes)
###

Chapter 33

Mom sits politely, if not cautiously, in the chair next to my writing desk. She folds her hands in her lap as if to keep them safe, keeping her fingers where she can see them, not letting them dangle out of sight beside her where who knows *what* could creep up from between the shadows and nip them right off.

The chair beside my desk is where visitors sit. I don't have many visitors. Mom comes by once a week, though lately she's found reasons why she can't make it, so it's been every couple of weeks or so. Soon she'll stop citing reasons and bimonthly visits will be the norm, and then she can start making excuses to miss a few of *those*, too.

Dr. Sheridan visits me, though it's less of a visit than a field inspection. She sits in the chair for what I'm supposed to think is small talk, randomly appearing a few times throughout the week in between my scheduled appointments to chat about the Civil War book I'm reading or last night's Sox game. Dr. Sheridan doesn't know shit about the Civil War, and even less about baseball.

In a way, I guess you could say I'm home, at least geographically speaking. I'm in Massachusetts, anyway—which is a hell of a lot closer to home than Burnham, California. I'm a long-term guest of what everyone here calls the "Amherst Campus," a branch of a larger system of state-run juvenile detention facilities for teens with various psychiatric disorders. If you've ever seen *One Flew Over the Cuckoo's Nest*, you'll have an idea of what this place is like. I'm not even joking. I've been here for a year and a half, and in a few months when I turn eighteen they're supposed to move me to an adult facility where I'll stay for for as long as they feel like keeping me. I'm not looking forward to that.

So Mom sits there, feeling unsafe and not sure of what to say. She's afraid of coming across like she's uncomfortable talking about everything that's happened, which she is, so she overcompensates by taking it head-on and won't shut up about it.

"Sometimes I feel like a lot of this is my fault," she says. "You and your imaginary friends, even when you were little, they were so important to you. You listened to them more than you listened to your father and me."

"It's not your fault, Mom."

"But I can't get it out of my head, this one time—you remember the Kryczeks, next door. They moved away when you were so young, I know, but there was this time when Pauline, Mrs. Kryczek, she brought you home after you'd wandered off..."

I knew this story better than I knew my phone number. I'd only heard it a thousand times during the trial, and a thousand more in the months since. "Yes, mom. You've told me the story—"

"And at the door Pauline says to me, she says, 'he was talking to himself out back by our pool, talking to nobody, and he was crying.' And I say to Pauline, I say, 'what was he crying about?' and she says to me, 'he was going on about how he can't swim and he'll drown if he goes in the pool. It was like someone was trying to push him in, force him to go into the pool, but there was nobody there.' And that's when I should have worried more, James. I should have done something."

"Seriously, Mom, you shouldn't have wor—"

"That's nonsense. I should have paid closer attention to what was going on. I just thought all boys had their imaginary friends, and I should have realized yours were much more serious than that."

I glance across the room to the foot of my bed, where Sunny sits imitating my mother with her hands folded neatly in her lap, sitting up straight with her perfect motherly posture, her mouth doing an exaggerated mime of everything Mom is saying. I try to pretend she's not there, but Sunny's *very* distracting.

"I talked to your father the other night," Mom says, "he got an offer for his book, finally. All those years of writing columns for lousy magazines that didn't recognize his talent, and it finally paid off. Good for him, is what I say."

I nod in agreement. That short biography of Kurt Gödel Dad had been working on that summer became a full-length manuscript after all the experts at my trial went on and on about my delusions and paranoia and psychosis and whatever. Dad really got into the Gödel story after that. Probably thought it would help him understand me, or at least help him understand me a *little* bit.

Which it didn't. But he did get a book out of it, and I'm happy for him. At least somebody came out of that whole mess a winner.

Your mom got her nails done and she's wearing perfume, Sunny notes from across the room. *She's trying to look sexy for someone. I bet she's giving it to Dr. Benton after she leaves today.* Dr. Benton is an elderly hunchbacked psychiatrist with a wart on his cheek who wanders the halls from midnight to eight in the morning. Nobody knows what he actually does around here. *I bet she meets him in the group counseling office and she lets him do whatever he—*

"—Publisher says first quarter of next year, so that's pretty good," Mom says. "Sooner than I would have expected."

"Yeah, me too," I say, though I didn't hear what it is I'm agreeing with, since Sunny was talking over most of it. "Good for Dad."

From the bed Sunny says, quietly but impossible to ignore: *You think right now Dayle and Luke are doing it, like in the afterlife? In purgatory or wherever? I think they are, I really do. I think he's boning her senseless with his rotting little–*

"Mom, you don't have to stay all afternoon, I know you have stuff you'd rather–"

--and she's loving every minute of it, she's squealing and growling and yelling his name, yelling LUUUUUUKE–

"–I won't take it personally if you want to head home."

–LUUUUUKE! Sunny closes her eyes and lets her head roll back, really getting into the moment as she acts it out, moaning Luke Pelletier's name, clawing at the blanket on the bed and arching her back.

Mom smiles uneasily and stands, taking her purse from the back of the chair and surveying the empty room. "I won't bother you, James. I know you need some quiet time to yourself to..." She struggles for the right word. "To heal. I'll come by next Wednesday, we can pick it up then."

I give her a hug and she hugs back tentatively, as though afraid I might just decide to keep her with me forever by putting a blade between her vertebra—something I have no interest in myself, but Sunny's brought it up numerous times over the last eighteen months.

Mom steps out quietly, closing the door behind her and leaving me here with Sunny, just the two of us together in this little room, alone with each other for the rest of our lives.

About the Author

Shandy Lawson is the author of the teen thriller and YALSA-nominee *The Loop*, published in 2013 by Disney-Hyperion Books. He lives in New York City and is represented by John Rudolph of Dystel & Goderich Literary Management. Visit him online at ShandyLawson.com.